The Stepsisters

#4 Sisters in Charge

Tina Oaks

SCHOLASTIC INC.
New York Toronto London Auckland Sydney

No part of this publication may be reproduced in whole or in part, or stored in a retrieval system, or transmitted in any form or by any means, electronic, mechanical, photocopying, recording, or otherwise, without written permission of the publisher. For information regarding permission, write to Scholastic Inc., 730 Broadway, New York, NY 10003.

ISBN 0-590-41300-7

12 11 10 9 8 7 6 5 4 3 2 1   8 9/8 0 1 2 3/9

Printed in the U.S.A.   01

First Scholastic printing, February 1988

Sisters
in Charge

The Stepsisters

CHAPTER 1

H*awaii?*" Paige Whitman stared at her father in dismay. "You and Virginia Mae are taking off for Hawaii for nine whole days and leaving me with . . . everything?"

She wasn't fooling William Whitman. Both father and daughter knew that by "everything" she was referring to her fifteen-year-old stepsister, Katie Summer Guthrie. The two younger girls, ten-year-old Megan Whitman and Mary Emily Guthrie, wouldn't be any trouble during their parents' absence. Ever since the recent wedding of Philadelphia lawyer William Whitman to journalist Virginia Mae Guthrie of Atlanta, Georgia, the ten-year-olds had melded together like butterscotch sauce on ice cream. They wouldn't be any trouble for Paige, and she knew it. What's more, she knew her father knew she knew it. Otherwise, why were his thick, dark eyebrows making bushy little arches over skeptical blue-gray eyes so like her own?

1

And she couldn't pretend that Tuck was the "everything," either. Her seventeen-year-old stepbrother could take care of himself. So, the only person left in the newly combined households of Whitman and Guthrie to fall under the heading of an unpleasant "everything" was Katie Summer. Disapproval emanating from her father sent chilly little fingers up and down Paige's spine. He was giving her *that* look. The one he gave her any time she so much as hinted that Katie Summer Guthrie wasn't perfect. The look was new to Paige. During all those years after her mother's death, he'd looked at Paige with pride. But not anymore. Now she was being compared constantly to Katie Guthrie, and she seemed to be coming in second far too often.

"What everything?" her father demanded, his mouth making a cynical little curve in his handsome face. "What awesome burden are we leaving you with?"

There . . . even that tone of voice was new to her. And it's all Katie's fault, Paige thought resentfully. She ran one long, slender hand through silky, straight, dark hair and thought bitterly, I've been *trying*. I have! And we haven't had a major crisis since Katie was unfairly suspected of helping Mike Lynch cheat at school to stay on the swim team. And none of that was *my* fault.

But Paige suspected her father was still angry with her for not falling under Katie's spell the way everyone else had. Sighing, Paige thought sadly, He can't understand why all that bubbly cheerfulness doesn't charm my legs right out from under me. He can't understand why that stupid

2

drawl sets my teeth on edge and why I'm not thrilled to pieces to suddenly have a gorgeous blonde sister who knows her way around boys as well as I know my way around a library. For a really brilliant lawyer, this man can be awfully dense sometimes!

"Well," she stammered, "this is a big house. Running it is a major responsibility." It was, indeed, a large yellow Victorian house sprawled across the top of a Philadelphia hill. Not large enough, though, Paige reflected briefly, to allow her a room of her own now that the Guthries had arrived. (And would she ever, ever think of them as Whitmans like herself? Not likely!) Sharing a room with anyone would have been difficult for a person as private as Paige. Sharing it with someone whose primary hobbies seemed to be collecting perfume and makeup sent her entire nervous system into a tailspin. There were times now when she felt like a violin whose strings had been pulled too tight.

"Paige," her father said patiently, "Miss Aggie will be here. She's even giving up her Sunday off. We'll make it up to her when we return. But while we're gone she'll be taking care of the house just as she always does." Bill Whitman, a tall, well-built man whose thick hair was just beginning to gray, leaned against the fireplace mantel. He kept a level gaze on her face.

She hated that tone in his voice. The last time she remembered hearing it B.G. (before Guthries) was when she was four and had smacked the little girl next door, who was plump and had golden ringlets all over her silly head, when she had

3

called Paige a "toothpick with teeth." He had delivered a blistering lecture she'd never forgotten. Even after she'd apologized to the girl, he'd spoken to her with a chill in his voice for several hours. She hadn't heard that chill in his voice since then. Until recently.

Why couldn't he understand how *she* was feeling? She was happy that her father had met Virginia Mae. And it was neat of him to have picked someone who played the piano, a personal love of Paige's, and who was as interested in writing as she was. Paige had no complaints about her father's choice in a wife. And Mary Emily was adorable and Tuck wasn't a bad guy. Katie Summer, though, was a different story. Besides, they were all practically strangers, weren't they? And they had invaded her house and were living in it and relaxing in it as if they'd always belonged there. Where did that leave *her*? In half a room, that's where! And the other half was occupied by, of all things, a neatnik! A neatnik flirt! A neatnik-flirt-butter-wouldn't-melt-in-her-mouth girl.

Paige had thought things would be different when he got married. She had envisioned herself and her father together easing the new family in gradually, the way they welcomed guests when they entertained. She would be, as she had been for years, the "lady of the house," and Katie would have to follow her lead. Even when her father had said, "We're going to be one big, happy family, Paige," the concept hadn't really penetrated her consciousness. She hadn't realized that the business of creating one family out of two

4

would change her entire life so drastically. Someone had slipped into her house and replaced her old life with a strange new one without consulting her.

It wasn't fair. None of it was fair. And the worst part was that she wasn't supposed to complain about any of it. Because that would mean they *weren't* "one big, happy family" and her father didn't want to hear that. The slightest hint that they weren't was what put that tone in his voice.

"Paige," the tone said now, "I asked you a question. There isn't anything here you can't handle, is there?"

She shook her head. They hadn't had a honeymoon. Everyone should have a honeymoon. "No, I guess not. But who's going to be in charge here? Someone should be."

"Tuck. He's the oldest. But I expect you to do everything you can to see that things run smoothly. You're used to this house and Miss Aggie, so it shouldn't be a problem for you."

Well, if I'm so used to this house, Paige thought resentfully, why aren't you putting *me* in charge? The prospect of being able to order around a certain blonde stepsister was tempting. On the other hand, would she really want the responsibility of being in charge? No, she wouldn't. If anything went wrong (and it probably would) she'd be blamed. The last thing in the world she needed right now was more blame. She was already beginning to feel as if her picture might be on a post office wall somewhere.

"Okay," Paige agreed with a shrug, "Tuck it is. He'll be fair."

Up went the eyebrows again. "Fair? Paige, I don't like the sound of that. Are you expecting trouble?"

Was he kidding? They hadn't had more than a few peaceful days since the Guthrie clan invaded. (If it occurred to Paige that perhaps a tiny part of the reason for that was that she still considered them "the Guthrie clan" instead of part of the Whitman clan, she pushed the thought away, not ready to face it.) "No, of course not, Dad. I just meant Tuck isn't the sort of person to order everyone around."

But that wasn't at all what she'd meant and she was sure her father knew it. Shaking his head, he left the room. Paige sank into a leather chair, stretching long legs in jeans out before her. She could hear Megan and Mary Emily on the back porch swing, while upstairs Tuck's stereo sent the faint strains of a Huey Lewis song drifting down to the first floor. Virginia Mae was out in the garden chatting with the last of the chrysanthemums and Miss Aggie was rattling pots and pans in the kitchen. Katie Summer, Paige decided, was probably in their room alphabetizing her makeup collection. That could take years!

If only her new stepsister were more like . . . well, like *her*. Then they could have nice long talks and they could share things and go places together. She'd always wanted a sister closer to her own age.

But Katie Summer was so . . . so different. The drawl alone made Paige suspicious about the

6

prospect of a serious thought ever sliding into the brain under those blonde curls. Still, except for that brief period when she'd needed tutoring, Katie seemed to do okay in school. And she was often very funny, and Paige didn't think it was possible to be funny if you were stupid.

Everyone else *liked* Katie Summer. That was the cruelest blow of all. And her popularity made Paige feel as if she were the only occupant in a very small boat. Much of the time now, she also felt as if someone had set her little boat adrift on a very cold and lonely ocean. Almost everyone who *met* Katie liked her. Even Jake Carson, law-student-to-be, who was taking a year off and working as handyman to the Whitman household before taking up his studies again. Once upon a time, Paige had pinned a lot of romantic hopes on tall, dark-haired, dark-eyed Jake. She still suspected that things might have worked out between her and Jake if only Miss Guthrie had stayed in the South where she belonged. But she hadn't. Instead, she was here, sharing a room with a tall, thin stepsister who wasn't a neatnik, wasn't a flirt, wasn't on the swim team, wasn't all that popular and . . . no longer had a shred of privacy in her own room!

Just as Paige jumped up and walked to the French doors overlooking the side yard, a voice called out, "Hi! Hear the great news?"

How a soft and gentle drawl could sound like fingernails scraping across a blackboard, Paige had yet to figure out. She turned around, knowing Katie Summer would be in the doorway.

She was. And looking, as usual, like a model,

7

her athlete's body enhanced by soft gray trousers, the glow in her cheeks heightened by the soft peach blouse she was wearing. Wouldn't you know, Paige thought angrily, she'd be wearing peach?

"What great news?" Paige asked flatly. Did the girl ever get a zit? Wasn't her blonde curly hair ever limp or greasy? Didn't she ever *slouch*? She was definitely the perfect advertisement for the fresh fruits and veggies she was forever munching on as part of her swim team training program.

Katie came into the room, smiling. "Mom and Bill's honeymoon. In Hawaii. Doesn't it sound fabulous?"

"Oh, that. Yeah, sure."

Katie frowned. "You don't sound too thrilled."

She is *not*, Paige vowed silently, going to be a better sport about this than me. One of the worst things that had ever happened to Paige had occurred when, in a moment of weakness, she'd switched a beautiful picture of Katie Summer for an atrocious one and printed it in the school newspaper's feature story on the swim team. She'd regretted it almost instantly (that wasn't the sort of thing she *did*), but it was too late. Everyone guessed that she'd done it on purpose, her entire family, and all of her friends, not to mention the entire student body at Harrison High. But through it all, Katie Summer had been the quintessential good sport, smiling bravely and telling all who would listen that Paige couldn't *possibly* have done such a thing on purpose.

Well, not *this* time. If Katie was all for this honeymoon trip, then Paige was, too.

She forced a laugh. It sounded like rain hitting a tin roof. "Well, I'd be a lot more thrilled if I were going along. But I guess I'll just have to wait to see Hawaii. I just hope they have a terrific time." And that was true enough. What was making her skin feel stretched too tight was what kind of time the *rest* of this new family was going to have for nine long days. Would World War III erupt? Could two stepsisters actually co-exist without benefit of adult referees? How many times had Virginia Mae or Paige's dad stopped an argument before it became full-scale war? Katie Summer might be mild-mannered, but she stood up for herself. And now, for nine whole days and nights, the referees would be thousands of miles away, leaving Miss Whitman in this corner and Miss Guthrie in that corner, totally on their own.

Well, *I'm* not going to start anything, Paige vowed silently. I've had just about enough of people looking at me like I'm the Wicked Witch of the West. Dad's right. Except for Tuck, I'm the oldest, and this is my chance to prove that I'm still as mature and responsible as Dad always thought I was.

"Oh, I'm sure they'll have a good time," Katie responded enthusiastically. "It's so romantic."

She uttered the word "romantic" in almost a whisper, her blue eyes dreamy.

Paige's teeth clamped together as if they'd just been stapled.

It was going to be a very long nine days.

CHAPTER 2

They had a family meeting after dinner that night. And Katie Summer reacted to the honeymoon news exactly the way she had with Paige earlier that day. "Isn't it wonderful?" she cried, a beautiful smile dancing across her face. "I think it's so romantic, don't you, Tuck?" turning to her seventeen-year-old brother.

He obviously didn't share her joy. Unlike Katie, he hadn't had advance notice of the trip. His lower jaw followed the same pattern of descent as Paige's had earlier.

"Are you serious?" was his response, directed toward his mother, who was seated beside her husband, facing their children. "You're leaving all of us alone in this . . . this zoo?"

Virginia Mae stiffened in her seat. Lovely in a pale lavender blouse and skirt, she focused almost-violet eyes on her unhappy son's handsome face. "Yes," she said in a level voice, "and we're leaving you in charge. You're the oldest. And," she added crisply, "please do not call this house a zoo. This is our home now."

Tuck groaned. He shook a head full of brown curls and looked at her with a mixture of hurt and anger in his eyes. "I call it the way I see it!" he said hotly. "And if you think I'm going to play umpire for the red team and the blue team here," waving one long arm toward Paige and Katie, "think again!"

"Tuck!" Bill admonished sharply, "Don't talk to your mother like that!"

Tuck shook his head again. "I don't believe this," he muttered, staring at the gleaming hardwood floor. "This is unreal."

Megan and Mary Emily cried in one mournful voice, "You're going away? Why can't *we* come?"

Tuck was able to curb his temper for a minute. "Don't you know anything about honeymoons?" he asked, his eyes twinkling. "Kids aren't invited."

Ten-year-old Megan's red curls bobbed up and down as she bounced in her seat, an unhappy expression on her face.

Paige couldn't bear the look of abandonment in Megan's eyes. "Cheer up, Meg," she said, forcing the words from her throat. "It won't be so bad. Just think, no grown-ups! We'll eat popcorn and pizza and hamburgers every night, and you won't have to make your bed."

Megan brightened up a little, and Virginia Mae shot Paige a grateful look and said in a light voice, "Well, I don't know about that. But I'm sure" — fixing Tuck with a meaningful gaze — "that you'll do just fine, now that you're all acquainted.

11

That's why we waited — to give you all a chance to get to know each other better before going off on our honeymoon." Only the firm grip she maintained on her husband's arm revealed the doubt lying behind her words.

He talked her into it, Katie Summer thought, suddenly not quite so sure that she would survive nine days and nights with Paige and no parents. She didn't want to leave us all alone, but she knows she and Bill should have a honeymoon. She knows I'm going to go nuts here with Paige, whose side of the bedroom looks like the county fairgrounds *after* the fair is over. If Paige had her way, they could easily become buried in nine days of no Virginia Mae to gently persuade her stepdaughter to "Pick things up a bit, Paige, dear, please." They'd become buried in mounds of newspapers and magazines and books and papers and half-eaten apples and wet towels and empty soda cans and wrinkled clothes, and never be seen or heard from again.

"Who's going to do the housework?" Katie asked Virginia, deliberately avoiding Paige's disapproving look, because *someone* had to ask the question.

"*All* of you," Bill answered firmly. "Miss Aggie will be here, of course, to perform her usual duties. But she'll go home after the evening meal as she always does, and it will be up to all of you to see that some sort of order is maintained while she's gone."

Katie shuddered, knowing what Paige's idea of "some kind of order" would be. They'd all be lucky if the entire bathroom floor didn't turn a murky green from being buried under a sea of sodden towels.

"Tuck," Bill said in a voice that clearly left no room for discussion, "I agree with your mother. As the oldest, you must be left in charge. But," he added quickly, "we expect your sisters to cooperate fully with you." His eyes went from Paige's face to Katie's and back again to his daughter's. "So I trust that your skills as an umpire won't be necessary."

Ignoring the doubtful expressions on the faces of the three older children, Virginia Mae smiled and told Megan and Mary Emily that they would be returning with presents for all. That cheered up the youngest ones a little, although Megan continued to look to Paige for reassurance. Paige tried. She forced herself to think of every possible cheerful aspect of having absent parents. It wasn't easy. Wasn't peace for nine days as unlikely as expecting Scarlett, their Irish Setter, to cohabit peacefully with Binker, the cat?

"One more thing," Virginia added as she stood up. "I know a thing or two about teenagers with absent parents," softening her words with a smile, "and there are to be *no* parties."

Katie's skin flushed a deeper peach, since she had at that very moment been wondering exactly how many people would fit in the living room.

"In fact," her mother added, reading Katie's expression, "I think it best if we just make a blanket rule that *no* visitors are to be allowed while we're gone. That makes it simple."

"Not even Ben?" Paige wailed, speaking of one of the editors on the school newspaper and the only boy she was currently interested in dating.

"Not even Jake?" Katie cried, speaking of one of the primary reasons Paige had immediately resented her upon her arrival, when the young handyman at the Whitman house had transferred a mild interest in Paige to a strong interest in Katie Summer. "Not even Sara or Trish or Diane or Nickie?" speaking of her new friends.

Virginia Mae shook her head. "No one. If I bend the rules for one or two, you'll stretch it to include the entire high school. Besides, you're all going to be too busy to entertain, anyway."

"We are?" asked a wide-eyed Paige, whose idea of housework was taking her plate into the kitchen after a late-night snack. Hadn't her father said Miss Aggie was going to be there? There couldn't be that much housework left for them to do, could there?

Virginia Mae got up and put a friendly arm around Katie's shoulders. "You'll survive all this," she said cheerfully. "I didn't say you couldn't go out. I simply said I want no guests in this house while we're gone. You can stand that for nine days, can't you?"

"Nine days," Tuck announced in a leaden voice, "can seem like a really long time." He pulled his long, lean frame up out of the chair. "Wars have taken place in that length of time. I had the chicken pox for nine days once and it felt like nine years."

"I had the chicken pox, too," Mary Emily announced. "I didn't have to go to school and

14

Mommy made fudge for me and read to me. *I* don't think nine days is so awfully long."

Everyone but Tuck laughed as they all filed out of the living room.

Paige didn't follow Katie Summer upstairs. Instead, she went to the phone in the empty kitchen and dialed the number of her best friend, Judy Belnap.

"Well, they're entitled to a honeymoon, Paige," Judy said when Paige's tale of woe had ended. "Besides, it's not like you're being abandoned. Won't Miss Aggie be there?"

"Yes. But she goes home after dinner. *We're* supposed to take care of things from that point on. If Katie Summer Suzy Homemaker has anything to say about it, we'll probably spend the whole nine days waxing and polishing and dusting tiny little objects."

That remark was followed by a moment of disapproving silence.

"Oh, that's right," Paige said in a cool voice. "I'm *lucky* to have a beautiful, popular stepsister. You keep telling me that, and I keep forgetting. Shame on me."

"Oh, Paige, cut it out! You make me sound about as sensitive as aluminum foil. I *do* understand. I know it's rough. I just think it's silly to *plan* on having trouble with Katie Summer. Your parents haven't even left yet, and you're already practicing your right hook. I can hear it in your voice."

Paige laughed. But when she turned away from the telephone a few minutes later, a frown pulled

15

dark, delicately-arched brows closer together. Maybe Judy was right. Why invent problems?

Ascending the stairs, Paige promised to change her tune. She would be so supportive of this trip, her father would stop using *that* tone of voice with her.

Then she walked into her bedroom to find Katie sitting on her own bed, one small girl on either side of her, both of them listening raptly as their older sister told them everything she knew about Hawaii.

She's trying to cheer them up, Paige realized with a flash of jealousy. Why didn't I think of that? Since her junior year began, she'd had little time for Megan's problems. Even when her little sister had come to her and asked for help, Paige had been so preoccupied with her own situation she'd been, unwilling to really listen. And she'd excused her guilt by telling herself this whole business of combining families had been much easier on the ten-year-olds than it had on the teenagers — one teenager in particular.

Now, watching Megan gaze up at Katie adoringly, Paige remembered with a pang when that look had been reserved for her alone. Katie had already taken so much that was hers: half her room, her importance in her father's life, and any chance she'd had of developing a relationship with Jake Carson. Was she about to snatch Megan away, too?

"C'mere, Meg," Paige said, taking Megan's slender wrist and pulling her to her feet.

Katie Summer, interrupted in mid-sentence, looked up in surprise, as did the two smaller girls.

"Paige, I was *talking*," Katie said quietly.

"Paige, I want to stay here with Mary Emily," Megan protested.

"Pa-aige!" Mary Emily cried, "where are you taking Megan?"

Feeling outnumbered, Paige shrugged, let go of Megan and walked stiffly to her own bed. Sweeping aside the clutter that hid it, she flopped down angrily, feeling very alone. All of her good intentions about being supportive of the Hawaii trip melted like makeup under hot lights. Watching from under lowered lids as Katie soothed the two girls she thought, it won't matter how hard I try, it won't be good enough. Miss Neat 'n' Tidy will take charge the second Virginia Mae and Dad have taken to the sky.

Depressed, Paige rolled toward the wall and closed her eyes in an attempt to sleep. But she was still wide awake when Katie's voice told the girls good-bye and sent them on their way. And she was still awake when that same voice called out tentatively, "Paige? You asleep?"

Paige's automatic response was that that had to be the dumbest question people could ask. "Yes," she answered clearly, "I am sound asleep."

Katie Summer giggled. "Okay, so it was a dumb question." Pushing blonde waves back from her face, she lay on her stomach across her neatly made bed. If she lived to be a thousand years old, she would never understand how Paige could stand the clutter surrounding her. Her side of the room always looked as if someone had just conducted a thorough search of the premises. Katie suppressed a second giggle. Rummaging

17

through Paige's things could be hazardous to one's health. You just never knew what might be lurking in those piles and bundles and layers of . . . stuff.

"I didn't mean to butt in with Megan," she said, wishing Paige would sit up and look at her. Talking to her stepsister was never easy. It was almost impossible when faced with the back of a long, lanky form topped by a sheet of silky hair. "I didn't know you were planning to talk to her about the trip. And I wanted to cheer up Mary Emily, so it just seemed to make sense to talk to both of them at the same time."

Slowly, Paige rolled over to face Katie. "It's okay," she said, meaning it. If Katie was willing to apologize, she wasn't about to turn her down. That was exactly the kind of thing her father had warned her about. "Just meet her halfway, Paige, that's all I'm asking," he'd said more than once. Well, why not? If they were going to make it through nine days of absent referees, they would have to cooperate with each other.

"So," she said, propping her head up on a pillow under her chin, "what were you telling Megan and Mary Emily about Hawaii? Never been there myself and don't know anything about it. Fill me in."

By concentrating very hard, she was able to listen without focusing on how really pretty her stepsister was.

CHAPTER 3

When Katie told her best friends Sara Nolan and Diane Powers about the planned trip, they sighed with delight. Sara's short blonde hair moved wildly about her heart-shaped face as she cried, "Parents out of town, wow! Party time! Great. No one's had a really good party in ages." Diane nodded and grinned. "And there's enough room in that big house of yours for a real blast!"

"Nope," Katie said firmly as they made their way through the between-classes crowd in the halls, "no party. No way. I'm real sorry, but that's orders from headquarters. I'm not even allowed to have company."

Her friends groaned.

"My mother laid down the law," Katie explained quickly. "No guests at all while they're gone." An unaccustomed frown appeared on her lovely face. "I guess she doesn't trust me."

"Of course she trusts you," Diane disagreed. She wasn't used to seeing Katie unhappy. That seemed more foreign than the lazy drawl, which Katie's friends found charming. "It's probably the rest of the student body that she doesn't trust."

"Or maybe it's that stepsister of yours," Sara offered. "Maybe your mother thinks she'd bring in some rowdy crowd and wreak havoc on your house."

Katie shook her head vigorously. "No, not Paige. She's not the type."

"No, come to think of it," Sara agreed, "she doesn't look like the party type. Anyway, your mom is probably right about not trusting the rest of the school. Although I, myself," she added solemnly, "have never trashed a house in my life, of course."

"Of course," Diane said in the same solemn tone. "Nor have I." She grinned. "But I've heard stories about certain members of the football team."

They had reached their next class and stood opposite the doorway, waiting for the bell to ring. "I've heard," Diane continued in a low voice, "that inviting Ed Thomas to a party is the same thing as inviting a wrecking crew."

"You mean our star quarterback doesn't mind his manners at a party?" Sara asked with a grin. The three girls weren't Ed Thomas fans and had never understood what Jennifer Bailey saw in him. Katie, who had once witnessed an attack on her brother by the football player, considered him "rude, crude, and totally Neanderthal."

Diane shook her head. "And why should a party be any different? Ed Thomas's manners make Attila the Hun look like Emily Post."

As the bell rang and they turned to enter the classroom, Sara added, "I've also heard that Ed Thomas doesn't wait for an invitation. So if I were you, I wouldn't mention the fact that your folks are going bye-bye. I wouldn't mention it to anyone. Except us, of course, because the word might get around and you wouldn't want that, believe me."

"I'll be careful," Katie said as they took their seats. "And thanks for the advice."

She could have mentioned it in Atlanta without worrying about gate-crashers. If there had been an Ed Thomas at her high school there, she'd certainly never run into him. Everyone she knew there was nice. And they minded their manners. *Always.* That was one of the reasons Tuck had fit in so well there, and had so many friends. And it was one of the reasons why he *didn't* fit in so well here. People just weren't as formal. Poor Tuck. Katie felt that he was beginning to resent Virginia for having raised him the way she had. But she could hardly have brought him up to be a slob like Ed Thomas, could she? Why would any parent want to do that? If they were still in Atlanta, Tuck's manners wouldn't be a problem, and Katie felt sure that Tuck often had that very thought.

But if you were still in Atlanta, a little voice reminded her, there wouldn't be any honeymoon trip because there wouldn't have been any wedding, and your mom would still have that sad, lonely look on her face, the one that showed up the day your dad took off for parts unknown.

Katie shook her head, startling the students around her. Their teacher, an older man with graying hair, frowned at her. She was obviously daydreaming. Still, he had recently attended a swim meet and been very impressed with the girl's strength and power. She was really quite good. But that was no excuse for inattention in class. He made a note opposite her name in a black book on his desk, and continued with the lesson.

Katie Summer knew she should be paying attention. She had to keep up her grades in order to stay on the swim team. But she couldn't stop thinking about the impending trip. Thoughts of what it would mean for her and Paige ran around in her head like horses on a carousel. Would they get along okay? Would Paige even try? Sometimes she did try. Katie could always tell when Paige was concentrating on being "nice." She always got a pained look on her face, as if her shoes were pinching her toes. It was usually right after she and her father had been closeted in the library. Katie had no trouble imagining the conversations that took place there. "Be nice to your stepsister, this is hard for her." How Paige must hate those lectures!

But, Katie reminded herself, she wouldn't need those lectures if she'd just give me half a chance. She's always so . . . stiff, like a knight guarding the castle. What is she so afraid of? I'm not going to take anything away from her.

Ah, but you already did, the little voice accused. You took Jake.

But Jake wasn't *hers*! Katie protested silently. I didn't even know she wanted him. How could I?

And he isn't mine, either, she thought glumly. Not really. He still thinks he's too old for me, even though he isn't, and he still thinks there's no future for us. You'd think I had proposed to him or demanded an engagement ring, when all I really want to do is have fun. Why does he have to make such a big deal about dating someone who's "only" a sophomore in high school? What's wrong with that? It's not like he's dating Mary Emily.

"Miss Guthrie," a voice cut into her thoughts, "your parents pay what some say are exorbitant taxes to pay for these classes. I'm sure they'd be very unhappy to learn that you're not attending in spirit."

Laughter echoed around an embarrassed Katie as she muttered, "Sorry, sir."

There! Just *thinking* about Paige got her into trouble.

After school, in the noisy, busy newspaper office, Paige was having the same trouble concentrating. The task at hand at that moment happened to be pasting-up a group of letters to the editor. Glancing over one that concerned the fifty-minute length of classes, she grinned. Ben Collins would pass this one to Laurie Harris, his co-editor. Not a patient person by nature, Ben was especially impatient with what he called "whiners." True, he would use every ounce of his apparently limitless energy to fight for a principle he considered important. But trying to shorten classes, Paige knew, wouldn't be a goal he considered worthwhile. The letter would go to Laurie to be answered.

She watched Ben from across the room as he argued with Jim Gordon. Mentally, she told him not to slouch. Slouching cut a full inch or more off his height, and she loved the fact that he was taller than she was. Not many boys in school were. As he argued, he repeatedly pushed his glasses up on his nose, almost as if he were doing so to prove a point. Thick, dark hair fell forward across his eyes, and he brushed it back as impatiently as he did everything else. She was sure they were arguing over some minor detail. But "minor details" were Ben's specialty. Which was, she knew, why their paper had won more awards than any high school newspaper in the city.

"Paige!" Ben called, "C'mere!"

Giggling softly, she said, "Yes, my lord and master, I hasten to do your bidding."

Of course he didn't laugh, or even crack a smile. "I know, I know," she said quickly, "this is serious business. So what's up?" Standing beside him, her boots bringing her up to his chin, she felt the same old shyness creep over her that always attacked her when she was near him. Ben was hard to figure out. He made no secret of the fact that he admired both Katie's looks and her swimming ability. When Paige had switched the gorgeous picture of Katie for an ugly one in a feature story they were doing on the swim team, he almost hadn't forgiven her. But it was the almost that counted. She *had* regained Ben's trust.

But she still wasn't completely relaxed around

him. She seemed to spend a lot of time waiting for that beautiful, warm smile to wash over Ben's thin, serious face. If the smile reached his hazel eyes, turning them greenish gold, she felt as if the sun had just come out after days of rain. But Ben wasn't the type who smiled easily. Life was too serious!

Ben waited until Jim had returned to his usual tasks before taking Paige by the elbow and leading her to his desk at the rear of the room.

"Busy tomorrow night?" he asked brusquely. The question was unheard by anyone but Paige amidst the clatter of typewriters.

She never hesitated when Ben asked her out. No coyness, no, "Gee, I'll have to check my schedule," no pretending she had to think about it. She had to think about many things these days: her relationship with this new family she was living with, her homework, her duties on the newspaper, what she wanted for a snack before bed, and what to wear to school each day. But she didn't have to spend one second's thought on whether or not she wanted to go out with Ben Collins.

"No," she said simply. "I'm not busy."

"Good!" he said heartily, pushing at his glasses. "We'll take in a movie. Pick you up at seven. Be ready. I don't like to — "

"Miss the beginning," she finished for him, smiling.

"Right." He didn't return the smile. "No point in seeing a film if you're going to miss the beginning." And he hurried off, but not before she noticed the flicker of surprise in his hazel eyes because she'd finished his sentence. He's surprised that I'm getting to know him so well, she thought to herself. Didn't he expect me to notice his likes and dislikes?

She hoped, as she returned to her work, that this wouldn't scare him off. She knew he had a hard time getting close to people. And she suspected that like her, he hadn't dated as much as some of the other kids in school.

Ben wasn't ready to leave when she was, but that failed to dampen her spirits. They had a date tomorrow night, and that made her happy. "See you later!" she called out to her co-workers as she left the office. They mumbled a response, heads bent over a sheaf of papers. Paige laughed as she left. It wasn't possible to feel jealous of Laurie, who was a coeditor with Ben. They were two of a kind: when Ben shouted, as he often did, Laurie shouted right back. Both employed sarcastic wit as effortlessly as other people said hello. Paige loved to listen to their arguments. It was like watching a play with really sharp dialogue. They were so equally matched, no one ever really won. The arguments just wound down and each went their separate way, looking triumphant. Then Ben would say casually, "Let's do it the way Laurie suggested," or Laurie would say the same thing about Ben's idea.

They were so much alike, Paige knew there was no question of a romance blossoming between them. Either their similarities would bore them to tears, or their continual struggles for power would undo them. Either way, she was positive Laurie was no threat to her.

She wished she could think the same thing about Katie Summer, she thought, as Katie came down the hall, fresh from swim team practice, judging from the way her dark blonde hair waved damply about her face and clung to the shoulders of her light-blue sweatsuit.

No one, Paige thought irritably, should look that good after two hours soaking in water. I'll bet her fingers aren't even wrinkled, she thought, and to her dismay her eyes darted to the small, strong hands holding an armload of books. She couldn't see Katie's fingertips.

"Hi, Paige. Headed home?"

They never, *ever* went home together. If Paige wasn't alone, she was with Judy or Ben. And Katie was usually centered in a small group of the new friends she'd collected since coming to Philadelphia.

"Yes." They began walking together. "Where's your fan club?" Why did every sentence she uttered to Katie Summer come out sounding snide?

But Katie just laughed. "They all gave up and went home. I don't know why they watch practice, anyway." She laughed again as they pushed open the heavy door and entered the crisp clear evening, not yet quite dark. "Well, that's not true. I do know why they watch practice. To watch the *guys*. But they all have tests tomorrow, so they went home to study." She groaned. "And I've got those same tests, so I know what *I'm* going to be doing tonight."

They talked about schoolwork, a safe topic, all the way home.

27

CHAPTER 4

No one was more surprised than Paige to discover that she felt bad when she left the house the following night with Ben, while Katie sat by the telephone, a look of yearning on her face. Paige knew what Katie was doing: she was waiting, hoping, wishing Jake would call. And the funny thing was, even though she still resented Katie for appropriating Jake, she felt sorry for her. Because Jake was proving to be really slippery. Paige had no idea why. He'd show up unexpectedly, whisk Katie off for an entire evening, and she'd come into the house later with a dreamy expression on her face. Then it might be weeks before Jake called or came around again, except to do the yardwork, and even then he'd make a point of leaving the Whitman property before Katie got home from swim practice. And Katie would gradually lose that dreamy-eyed look.

Yet Paige had seen the two of them exchanging a kiss in the backyard, and Jake had certainly seemed to mean that kiss. So why was he dragging his feet with Katie Summer? It must be so maddening for her.

Well, it wasn't Paige's problem. Besides, she thought as she climbed into Ben's father's sedan, Katie Summer could have any boy she wanted at school. She could pick and choose among the best of them. It's not *my* fault she wants Jake, Paige thought as Ben started the car. Let *her* figure out what to do about it.

But every once in a while during the evening, the picture of Katie sitting by the telephone flashed across her mind. She wondered if Jake had called.

Jake hadn't called. But Paige needn't have worried, because Katie did *not* sit by the telephone all evening. She liked Jake. She liked him a lot. But she was tired of feeling like a yo-yo. He wound her up and then let her fall. All because of something as silly as a few years' difference in their ages and something he called his "life plan." Life plan? Ridiculous! She was sure Jake liked her. She could tell about things like that. And he did keep boomeranging back to her, usually when she least expected it. But she wasn't going to spend a perfectly good Friday evening sitting around waiting to catch a boomerang.

She went to the movies with Lisa and Sara. After the movie, they walked to Smokey Joe's, a barbecue restaurant they all liked. Five minutes after they arrived, Diane and her date walked through the door. Lisa waved them over to the booth. Katie whispered, "We shouldn't butt in," but Lisa brushed aside her objections, saying, "Don't be silly. She's not that crazy about the guy. We'll be rescuing her. And maybe they'll give us a ride home. Remember," she added, "don't say word one about your parents' trip. This guy could have a big mouth."

She needn't have worried. Katie's friends had thoroughly convinced her that mentioning the trip would be a major mistake.

But just as Diane and her date reached the booth, Lisa pointed to the front of the restaurant and asked, "Katie, is he looking for you?" Katie looked, expecting to see Tuck and saw instead . . . Jake Carson. He was standing alone in the doorway and he was looking, unsmiling, straight at Katie Summer.

Uncertain, she remained where she was. While it was clear that Jake was there looking for her, she had no intention of running over to him like a puppy claiming its owner. If he'd wanted to see her tonight, why hadn't he picked up the telephone and asked her out like a normal person?

She waved casually. Then she turned to Lisa and pretended to begin a conversation. And by fastening her eyes securely on the sugar dispenser, she was able to avoid looking at Jake. But not before she'd noticed how great he looked: dark hair brushed neatly, crisp khaki slacks, white shirt, sleeves rolled to the elbows. His jawline was set with the intensity that both frightened and intrigued her.

"Hang onto your hat," Lisa murmured, head lowered over her Coke, "here he comes."

Katie Summer made no reply, but her body

stiffened with resolve. If he intended to claim her like a coat left at the dry cleaners, he was in for a surprise.

"Hi, there," Jake said casually as he arrived at their booth. The girls greeted him in one voice. Then there was an awkward moment of silence before he followed up with, "Katie Summer, can I see you for a sec?"

She looked up at him, her fingers lazily shredding her straw wrapper. "Oh, gee, Jake, I'm sorry," she drawled, "but I wouldn't want to be rude to my friends."

Jake's jaw tightened and he stood up straighter. But to Katie's chagrin, Lisa burst out with, "Oh, that's okay, Katie. We won't mind."

So much for my good intentions, Katie thought grimly. It was hard to stick to your guns when your best friend was a hopeless romantic. Without uttering one exasperated word to Lisa, she slid out of the booth and followed Jake outside.

"You're not an easy person to track down," he said, leading her to his car in the parking lot. "I've been all over town."

She was not going to make this easy for him. "Jake, we always come here after a movie." He shrugged and leaned against the car. "Well, I didn't know you were *at* a movie. When I called, Mary Emily just said you'd gone out. I figured maybe you had a date."

Thank you, Mary Emily, Katie thought. She looked up at him. "And if I'd been with a date instead of my friends, what would you have done?"

Jake grinned. Katie's heart went out of action

temporarily. "Told the guy to get lost, I guess. What's the difference? You weren't *with* a date."

"No, but I could have been." That was true enough. A boy in her English class had asked her out. She'd said she was busy because she'd been hoping Jake would call. Well, she wasn't going to do that anymore. She *wasn't*. Then maybe the next time he came looking for her, he would find her with a boy. Maybe then he'd stop treating her like a convenience store, dropping by whenever he felt the need for a little adoration. Which, of course, he wasn't going to get tonight. He should consider himself lucky that she'd even spoken to him. If it hadn't been for Lisa, she wouldn't have.

He grinned again. "I don't doubt that for a second. The boys at Harrison High must be lined up around the block waiting for you to flash your famous smile at them."

Well, that wasn't exactly true. It was hard being "the new girl." Some of the boys (and more than a few of the girls) didn't trust her accent. She had no idea why. She preferred it herself to their thin, nasal-sounding syllables. *She* would never let something as trivial as how a person spoke get in the way of finding out about them. Apparently there were a lot of kids here who didn't feel the same way.

"Right." But Katie Summer didn't allow herself to return Jake's grin. It disappeared. "Well," she said, her voice cool, "you dragged me out here. What do you want?"

"I want to give you a ride home. We need to talk."

She said nothing. It seemed so easy for him.

32

He just showed up, looking positively wonderful, and expected her to fall into his arms. Well, she'd shave her head first!

Then he said, "Please, Katie?" and she opened the door and got into his car.

They didn't really straighten out their situation. Parked on a hill overlooking the long ribbon of river, they discussed, for what seemed to Katie to be the thousandth time, Jake's plans. He would be going away to college, then on to law school. He would be busy. No time to write letters or sit for hours dreaming about a girl who hadn't even finished high school yet. Most especially, no time to "get involved."

Katie didn't feel like having this discussion again. "Then don't," she said lightly, even as her heart protested.

"Don't what?" Jake frowned at her. They were sitting close together on the front seat. If she'd wanted to, she could have reached up and wiped away the frown with her fingers. She didn't feel like it.

"Don't get involved."

He looked hurt.

She giggled. "I declare, you look like someone just said there isn't any Santa Claus. I was just agreeing with you, Jake."

"I don't want you to agree with me. You never did before."

Katie Summer nodded. "I know. But I'm tired of the same old argument. I don't want to *marry* you, Jake, I told you that before. I don't know who you're trying to convince with all this arguing — me or you."

Jake thought about that for a minute, even as his arm went around Katie's shoulders and pulled her closer. He decided it would be a big mistake to tell Katie that the reason he kept going over the same ground was that he thought about her practically every waking moment. Handling that was getting rougher all the time. He'd had his master plan mapped out for a long time, and he'd been happy with it. Then this beautiful girl with the lazy drawl and blue eyes that seemed to see right through him had shown up and his master plan became just so much shredded wheat.

"Okay, you're right," he surrendered. "Let's not talk about it anymore."

Katie smiled to herself. They'd talk about it again, she was as sure of that as she was that Jake's arm around her shoulders felt more comforting than freshly-baked chocolate chip cookies. She might not belong in Philadelphia or in the yellow Victorian Whitman house, but she certainly belonged in Jake Carson's arms, whether he knew it or not.

"My parents are going to Hawaii," Katie said, gratefully changing the subject. "On a delayed honeymoon trip."

"Oh, yeah? Your grandmother coming to stay with you?"

Honestly. Did every remark out of that handsome mouth of his have to imply that she was still wearing braids and knee socks?

"No, my grandmother isn't coming to stay with us," she answered hotly. "Our parents trust us, Jake." Then she added, less angrily, "And Miss Aggie will be there."

34

"Maybe I ought to hang around a little more," he suggested thoughtfully. "I could come every day. Just in case — "

"Just in case what?" He *did* think she was a baby! "Jake, we're all grown-up people. We can take care of ourselves."

He laughed, then. "Yeah, I guess you're right. Maybe I was just looking for an excuse to see you more often."

"You don't *need* an excuse. Anyway, I'm not home when you're doing the yardwork, now that I've got swim team practice. But," Katie grinned, "I'm sure you could come over and do more chores for Miss Aggie. She'd appreciate that." She thought for a minute and then added softly, "Don't you think a Hawaiian honeymoon sounds romantic?"

And Jake bent his head then to show her, with warmth and affection, his own notion of what was romantic.

Paige and Ben, sitting on the back porch swing after their movie, were discussing the "romantic" honeymoon trip, too. But Paige was careful not to express her annoyance at being left alone with Katie Summer.

But Ben Collins didn't get to be coeditor of the school newspaper by being obtuse. He listened silently as she forced enthusiasm into her voice and described the upcoming trip. She thought she did rather well, and finished on a note of smug self-satisfaction, "And I know they'll have a terrific time."

Ben looked at her and said matter-of-factly,

"And you're wondering how you and Katie Summer are going to survive the nine days."

She stared at him, open-mouthed. "I didn't say one word about Katie Summer!"

He smiled and took her hand in his bony one. "I know you didn't say a word about her," he said, "and I think that's great. If you go into this nine-day thing with a great attitude like that, it should be a breeze."

Paige suddenly felt guilty. Ben thought she had an open mind about the trip, and she was *letting* him think it. But telling him she dreaded spending that time with Katie would bring on the lecture she had just avoided. Anyway, she rationalized, hadn't someone once told her that if you told yourself that you could do something often enough, you really *could* do it? If she could convince Ben that she intended to truly make an effort to get along with Katie, maybe she could even convince herself.

"Yes," she said, leaning her head against his shoulder, "I think you're right. I think it's going to be a breeze. I do."

Ben laughed and reached up to tilt her chin toward him. "Don't protest too much," he said, smiling. "You do have a tendency to overdo things, don't you?"

Before she could answer, he bent his head and kissed her, a cool, firm kiss that deepened in intensity as she responded warmly.

By the time he lifted his head, she had decided that nine days alone with Katie Summer was going to be a piece of cake. Because all was right with the world.

CHAPTER 5

The following week was spent preparing for the trip. Megan and Mary Emily walked around with long, doleful faces until Virginia Mae cheerfully reminded them that she'd be bringing back souvenirs. On Saturday afternoon Tuck agreed to take the two younger girls to the park a short distance from the house, leaving his mother free for a last-minute shopping trip with Paige and Katie Summer.

But they hadn't been in the department store long before Katie began wishing she'd stayed home. Reading a good book or listening to music, even cleaning her room or brushing the cat would be better than this. Because it quickly became apparent that Paige and Virginia Mae were going to share their interest in conservative, tailored clothing in muted, classic colors, while Katie preferred more contemporary clothing in bright colors, clothes designed with style and wit. It didn't take long for her to begin feeling like a fifth wheel.

The first time she saw an outfit she thought would be perfect for a trip to Hawaii, she pointed it out with enthusiasm. And flushed scarlet with embarrassment as her mother and Paige exchanged a look of amusement and rolled their eyes upward. Fury boiled up inside of Katie Summer. This wasn't the first time she and her mother had disagreed on choice of clothing. But it had always been *Katie's* wardrobe they'd argued about, not Virginia Mae's. And there hadn't been a tall, thin outsider in navy blue skirt and blazer over a white tailored blouse to side with Virginia Mae. That really hurt.

"Well, *I* think it's pretty," Katie stammered defensively.

Virginia Mae smiled. "Yes, you would think that, dear," patting Katie's arm.

I am *not*, Katie thought angrily, two years old. I don't need to be humored. And that superior smile on Paige's face definitely needed to be slapped off. Good thing the Guthries were basically nonviolent. So her mother and Paige shared the same taste in clothing. Big deal. No reason for Paige Whitman to look as if she'd just scored one hundred on a difficult exam.

"You know, Paige," Katie said clearly as they bypassed the flowered gown and moved on to more conservative clothing, "you and Mom may have the same tastes, but you sure *treat* your clothes differently." She paused to make sure Virginia Mae was listening before adding, "*She* hangs *hers* up!"

38

"Katie!" her mother scolded gently, "that's not very nice." Paige, who had scowled at the remark, looked smug again.

Katie shrugged. "No, but it's true. Paige doesn't really *need* her half of the closet. She likes to use her clothes as a carpet."

"That's enough, Katie Summer," Virginia Mae said sternly. She had wondered about this outing. Taking both girls with her seemed risky. But the last time she'd gone somewhere with Paige, Katie's feelings had been hurt. She didn't want to put either girl in a hostile frame of mind any time, but especially not right now. And she had hoped that a shared shopping trip would bring them closer together. Now that seemed like a futile hope. Didn't the two of them ever agree on anything?

"I'm starving," Katie said.

"Me, too!" Paige agreed, answering Virginia's unspoken question. And although they hadn't yet accomplished anything, Virginia Mae wasn't about to ignore their willingness to do *something* together, even if it was something as trivial as lunch.

The lunch, eaten in an Early American restaurant brightened by bouquets of autumn flowers, went well. Although talk centered mainly on the upcoming trip, they did talk briefly about what was going on in each girl's life at school. Katie talked about the swim team and several of her classes. Virginia Mae listened attentively, making warm comments from time to time as she spooned fruit cocktail from a sherbet dish. So when Paige began talking enthusiastically about the news-paper and Virginia Mae, a journalist, seemed just a shade more interested, Katie refused to let jealousy overtake her. It made sense that her mother would be more interested in Paige's newspaper work. Ignoring them, she turned her attention to her club sandwich.

After lunch, Katie and Paige browsed through the Junior section while Virginia Mae tried on several dresses. Taking advantage of her absence, Katie did some experimenting on her own. While Paige couldn't bring herself to say so aloud, she admitted silently that Katie Summer had more style than any girl she knew. Maybe it was because she really enjoyed clothes. Paige didn't think clothes would make that much difference in the way she looked. As long as she was neat and clean and the colors she chose suited her dark hair and fair skin, she felt she looked okay. But Katie was much more adventurous with clothing. She picked outfits that seemed to suit her personality as much as her coloring. By adding a brightly-colored scarf or a wide belt to pieces she had mixed and matched, she achieved totally different looks.

Now, Katie danced before her, wearing a blue denim miniskirt, matching blue boots and cap, and a crop-top of white lace with long sleeves and high collar. You do not wear lace with denim, Paige told herself and then changed her mind. On Katie it looked not only right, but charming. With the cap perched at an angle on her wavy blonde hair she looked, Paige thought, like an actress or model. And for just a second, she felt sympathy for Katie, thinking it was a shame that

40

Virginia Mae didn't let her daughter pick out more of her own clothes.

But when Katie, staring at herself in a full-length mirror, wailed, "Oh, this looks so great! If only Mom — " Paige interrupted with a flat, "She'd never let you wear a skirt that short." She wasn't sure why she cut Katie off so abruptly. Maybe it was because the girl just looked too super.

"I know," Katie said, disappointment heavy in her voice. "But *lots* of girls are wearing short skirts, especially denim ones."

"You're not lots of girls," Paige reminded her in Virginia Mae's voice.

Katie looked up and giggled. "You sounded just like her. I guess now you're going to tell me to 'get those things off and look for something more ladylike,' right?"

Paige returned the grin. "You do look terrific," she said generously.

"Oh, Paige," Katie begged, "maybe you could talk her into it. She trusts your judgment. Couldn't you give it a whirl?"

Paige shook her head. A blanket of soft dark hair swirled around her cheeks. "No way. She'll say no, anyway, but she'll be mad at both of us if I ask. I don't want her leaving in that kind of mood." Then she couldn't resist adding sternly, "And you shouldn't, either."

Katie knew she was right. "Okay," she said heavily. "I'll go put on my stupid gray pants and my stupid pink sweater. But I won't be happy about it!"

Paige laughed. "You don't have to be happy about it. You just have to do it. And fast, because that looks like your mother coming toward us now."

Katie gasped and made a dash for the nearest dressing room.

When they got home, Megan and Mary Emily were still occupied with the business of "dressing up" in their mother's clothes. Mary Emily had wrapped herself up in a two-piece gray suit, the skirt dragging along the floor, the jacket held on with a brown leather belt, while Megan was happy in a pale print dress topped with a blue cardigan sweater. When Paige saw them, she nudged Katie's elbow and whispered, "*You* might not agree with Virginia Mae's taste in clothing, but they seem to like it just fine."

Katie laughed softly as Virginia Mae handed each younger sister a new book of stickers. "What do *they* know about fashion?" Katie whispered with a grin. "They're only ten!"

Bill Whitman took them all out that night to a "farewell" dinner at a well-known restaurant in the area. They were given a large round table close to the stone fireplace that held a huge basket filled with rust and yellow chrysanthemums. From this vantage point, Katie and Paige were able to see all the guests coming in and leaving.

A young woman in a red dress entered the restaurant and stood near the hostess's desk, looking around the room. Long blonde hair rested in thick waves on her shoulders and the expression on her beautifully made-up face was aloof.

"Wow, not bad!" Tuck exclaimed. "I wonder if she needs an escort."

Paige hooted. "Not likely. She *is* gorgeous, isn't she? If you like the Hi-I'm-just-slumming type."

"She *is* pretty," Katie said, a wistful note in her voice. "So . . . sophisticated. And look at that dress!" She directed an annoyed glance at her mother. "I saw one just like it in a magazine last week. *Some* girls are allowed to wear fashionable clothes."

Virginia Mae smiled. "Some girls," she said, "are older than you are. That young woman is at least eighteen. And you're not."

"You sound like Jake," Katie grumbled, reaching for a roll.

"Look!" Tuck exclaimed in a surprised voice and all heads at his table turned to follow his eyes.

The girl's date had arrived and was standing beside her, bending his head to tell her something. The girl's date was Jake Carson.

No one said a word. Katie's blue eyes were round as marbles, her mouth open in a disbelieving O.

"Probably his sister," Tuck volunteered, regretting having called everyone's attention to the new arrival.

"He doesn't *have* a sister," Katie said in a dead voice.

"Well, a cousin then."

"What's the matter with Katie Summer,

Mommy?" Mary Emily asked in a clear voice. "She's a funny color."

"Hush, dear," Virginia Mae cautioned. Then to Katie, softly, "Don't jump to conclusions. You can get hurt doing that."

Katie stared at her plate, visibly forcing back tears.

Paige felt terrible for her. She knew how she would feel if Ben had walked in with another girl. "She's probably just an old friend, Katie. Someone he knew in high school."

Katie nodded, eyes still on her plate. "Right. Someone more his age," she said bitterly. And she was thinking, But what about last night? Didn't he mean anything he said? Didn't he mean anything he did? Had he kept silent about this date tonight because he didn't think it was any of her business? After all, he hadn't made any promises to her. If anything, he'd been trying for a long time to convince himself that he didn't really want her. Was that what he was doing tonight? Was this just another part of his effort to convince himself that he'd be better off with someone older?

The horrid knowledge that he was going to see her at any moment crept over her. If only she could crawl under the table. Katie could feel the hurt etched across her face. She would die before she would let Jake Carson see that. She couldn't let him see how much power he had to hurt her.

"He's coming over here," Paige whispered, kicking at Katie's foot under the table to get her attention. "Look happy!"

Katie snapped into action, using every ounce of

44

will power she possessed. It's just like swimming that last lap, she told herself sternly. You always think you simply cannot do it, and you always *do* it. You can do this, too!

Jake at least, she realized with a tiny bit of satisfaction, had the decency to look embarrassed as he and the girl stopped at the Whitman table.

"Hi," he said, looking from one face to another in search of support. Getting none, his eyes made their way to Katie's face. She was smiling and her eyes were dangerously bright. He knew that look, and wished fervently that he'd told her last night he'd made this date a week ago, when he had been very discouraged about their chances together.

"Hi, Jake!" she said crisply. "I'm surprised to see you here." But her expression clearly said, You may both drop dead this instant.

Not at all fooled by her greeting, Jake had no choice but to introduce the girl, who stood at his side looking bored. "I'd like you all to meet Sandra Taylor. We went to high school together. My father and hers work together downtown."

Paige kicked Katie again. See? the kick seemed to say, I told you she was someone he went to school with. Katie didn't see what difference it made where the girl had come from. It was where she was *now* that seemed important. She was with Jake. And Katie wasn't.

The adults politely acknowledged the introduction as the girl in the red dress said a lazy, "Hullo."

"We're just here for dinner," Jake said unnecessarily.

Paige couldn't resist. "No kidding? We thought you came for the bowling."

The girl looked surprised. "They have *bowling* here?"

Paige laughed, and Katie giggled. "Guess who didn't graduate at the top of her class?" Paige whispered.

"No," Jake said in a tense voice, "they don't have bowling here. She was just kidding." His dark eyes threw daggers directly at Paige, and Katie suspected she was included in his aim, too. She didn't care. He had it coming!

The girl looked bored again. And Katie thought, Aw, too bad.

"C'mon, let's go," he said, tugging on the elbow of the red dress. He didn't add, We're not wanted here, but Katie heard it in his voice and was glad.

But as she watched him lead Sandra to a corner table, her blue eyes looked so sad, Paige had to fight an impulse to pat Katie's arm in comfort.

Then she thought, Watch it! You're going to begin really feeling sorry for her.

And Katie did indeed look very much alone as she picked at the food on her plate.

CHAPTER 6

Virginia Mae and Bill left the house the following afternoon, going by taxi to the airport. "Silly
for you to drive us," Bill told Tuck. "It's just as
easy to take a cab, and I'd rather you stayed here
with the girls."

Tuck gave "the girls" a disgusted look, but
quickly assured his parents one more time that
they would all be "just fine," in spite of the unhappy looks on the faces of Megan and Mary
Emily. Katie's expression of unhappiness he paid
no attention to at all, knowing it had more to do
with Jake's appearance last night than with their
parents' disappearance today.

"If you want to worry about something," Tuck
joked as they all gathered on the wide front porch
to say good-bye, "worry about one of those volcanoes erupting while you're over there."

Megan's face paled. "Daddy!" she cried, clutching at her father's jacket sleeve, "you're not going to go near any volcanoes, are you?"

"No, of course not, pumpkin," he said, bending down to give her a bear hug. "We're just going to lie on the beach and relax."

"And go shopping?" Mary Emily reminded her mother.

Virginia Mae laughed. "Yes, of course. We won't forget your presents, darling. Now, remember, you girls mind your brother. And your older sisters. Promise?"

They nodded solemnly, although Megan still hadn't regained her normal coloring.

"And you older ones," Bill Whitman said firmly, "know what we expect from you." His eyes were on Paige's face. She forced a look of total innocence. "I trust we won't be disappointed."

The cab arrived and began honking before any of the three could make any more promises. Giving hugs all around, the adults descended the stone steps to the waiting cab. Tuck accompanied them, luggage in hand. The others waited on the porch, prepared to wave good-bye. Paige had an arm around a sad-faced Megan, while Katie held Mary Emily's hand in her own. They all watched silently, waving, as the taxi pulled away. Then Tuck ran back up the steps, greeting them with a cryptic, "Family meeting. Kitchen. Now!"

Paige and Katie exchanged exasperated glances. Couldn't Tuck at least wait until the cab was out of sight before ordering them around? But they followed him into the house. Neither girl wanted to get off on the wrong foot with him.

They both knew he could be a formidable foe when angered.

Miss Aggie was clearing up the last of their Sunday meal as they all piled in and sat down.

"Folks get off all right?" she asked, brushing back a wisp of graying hair that had escaped the hairnet she always wore when working. She wiped plump, freckled hands on the apron worn over her gray cotton dress and waited for an answer.

Tuck nodded. "Now," he told her, "we need to work out a plan of action so you don't have to do everything by yourself."

Miss Aggie nodded approvingly. Paige went into the dining room and sat down, followed by Katie and the little girls, then Tuck. As Mary Emily took the top off the salt shaker and peered inside, Megan asked in a quavering voice, "Tuck, how often do volcanoes erupt in Hawaii?"

Ignoring her, Tuck said a bit sharply, "Everybody please pay attention." Paige and Katie sat up straight in their chairs. Mary Emily replaced the salt shaker top and folded her hands in her lap. Megan bit her lower lip.

Tuck got up to pull several sheets of paper and a pencil from a cupboard drawer. Resuming his seat, he said heartily, "Now! Here's what we need to do. We need to make lists of everything that needs to be done. That's first. Then we need to decide who's going to do them."

Miss Aggie nodded again before returning to the kitchen. But Paige said plaintively, "Oh, Tuck, don't make such a big deal out of this. What's to do? Unload the dishwasher every morning and fold a few clothes. Those are hardly major

49

undertakings. It's not as if *Better Homes and Gardens* is coming to do a full-color spread on the Whitman home."

"Oh, my goodness, Paige," Katie burst out, "there's a lot more to keeping a house clean than folding clothes." She hadn't heard the first part of Paige's declaration because she'd been wondering if Jake Carson was taking the blonde girl out again that night.

"She's right, Miss," Miss Aggie said as she passed behind Paige with an armload of clean towels. "And Tuck's got the right idea. Organization is the key, I always say. A place for everything and everything in its place, that's the way to do it."

Paige's eyes turned from velvety brown to hard, dark marbles. Was Miss Aggie going to be on Katie's side the whole nine days? And did Miss Domestic Engineer of the Year have to look so smug? Remembering her promise to her father, Paige sighed in surrender and told Tuck to go ahead with the list. "But I am *not*," she said firmly, "cleaning the bathrooms."

"We noticed," Katie quipped. Tuck grinned.

Paige glared at each of them. "I mean every *day*!" she said hotly.

"I meant *any* day," Katie murmured.

"Okay, you two, cut it out," Tuck ordered. "Now, let's get this over with. If anybody thinks of anything that needs doing, spit it out, and I'll jot it down."

"We're not allowed to spit," Mary Emily protested. "Mommy says spitting is for leaky faucets and outboard motors and that's *all*."

50

Tuck didn't laugh. "Never mind."

"Actually," Katie said slowly, "I think Paige is right."

Astonishment slid across Paige's face. Katie Summer might just as well have said, "I think Paige is wonderful." The effect would have been the same.

"I mean," Katie continued, "with Miss Aggie here, except in the evenings, we really *don't* have all that much to do. We just need to clean up any mess we make in the evening, that's all." The truth was, she wasn't interested in this list-making business. It seemed unimportant. She was anxious to get up to her room, where she could lie on her bed and wonder what was going to happen between her and Jake.

Paige nodded with satisfaction. She even managed a tiny smile aimed somewhere in the vicinity of her stepsister. No point in going overboard with gratitude.

Tuck looked doubtful. "You really think it's that simple? This is a big house and I don't want Mom and Bill coming home to a mess."

Katie shrugged. "Neither do I. But we all know what a wonder Miss Aggie is." Then she added hastily, "Not that we won't help. We will. I think Paige and I are just as much in charge as you are, Tuck. Anyway, since Mom said no visitors, our social lives will be so quiet, we'll have plenty of time to help. Especially *my* social life," she finished quietly.

"Well, she didn't say we couldn't go *out*," Tuck said, "so I don't expect *my* social life to be all that dead. And speaking of going out, curfew is the same as it always is. Ten on school nights, twelve on weekends. Got that?"

Paige nodded. "No problem. We're used to it. Doing things any differently would feel funny."

Not to me it wouldn't, Katie thought to herself. It might be fun to come in late just once. And Jake might not see her as being so much younger without that stupid curfew. Then she remembered that Jake hadn't even called to explain about the blonde in the red dress, so why was she wasting time thinking about him?

"Okay," Tuck said, giving in, "if you don't think we need lists, then I guess that's it for tonight. But," he added as chairs scraped away from the table, "any time I think we've got problems, I'm calling another meeting."

"Yes, *sir*!" Paige said with a grin and a snappy salute. "Whatever you say, sir!"

Tuck was not amused. He was taking his responsibilities very seriously. It was his intention that when his parents returned from Hawaii, the house would look exactly as it had when they left. No soda stains on the hardwood floors. No broken windows or furniture. No ceiling stains from an overflowing bathtub, no dirty dishes in the sink. And *no* clutter! His mother hated clutter.

Katie and Paige seemed to think it would be easy. He hoped they were right.

During the next few days, he decided they had been. Little changed in their regular routines. The absence of adult voices during the evening was the only noticeable difference in the house. They helped out in the kitchen after dinner so that Miss

Aggie could go home at a decent hour, but they often did that even when their parents were home. And they were careful to clean up any mess they made during the evening each night before going to bed, so that the house would pass Miss Aggie's inspection the following morning.

"Um-humm," she murmured each day as she surveyed the kitchen, free of dirty dishes, opened cookie boxes, and empty milk cartons or soda cans. "Not bad, people, not bad," she praised three mornings in a row.

One family rule that Tuck had refused to suspend was the one about the entire family being available for dinner. "If it was just us," he told Paige and Katie, "I'd drop it for now. But there's Miss Aggie. She's doing the cooking, and we all know she won't go home until we've all eaten. So I think we should all stick to the routine."

Paige and Katie agreed, although they had both been looking forward to a temporary suspension of that particular rule. It was hard, watching the clock each afternoon in the newspaper office or at the school pool, making sure they wouldn't be late. It would have been nice to relax a bit.

Paige especially thought it was important for the two younger girls to have their evening routine undisturbed. Megan still seemed a bit pale and listless, in spite of Mary Emily's valiant efforts to cheer her up. Her playtime each evening was spent as close to the telephone as possible. When her parents called to say they'd arrived safely in Hawaii, she seemed temporarily more like her old self. But by the next day, she was once again anxiously eyeing the calendar on the kitchen wall, x-ing off the vacation days with a fat red Magic Marker.

Paige made up her mind to talk to Megan. She was obviously missing her parents a lot. But shouldn't she have snapped out of that by now? Mary Emily certainly wasn't moping around. Why wasn't Megan following her example? Deciding Megan just needed a little reassurance, Paige made a mental note to talk with her younger sister as soon as she could find the time.

But she was very busy at the newspaper, running errands for Ben, doing pasteups for Laurie, even coming up with a new idea occasionally. By the time she arrived home each evening, she felt as if she'd just run a marathon. The last thing in the world on her mind was her younger sister's worried face.

Katie, still preoccupied with what she considered Jake's betrayal, made a special effort to make it home every night. She told herself it was so she wouldn't be late for dinner, but she knew in her heart it was in hopes of catching Jake before he left for the day. But now that it was fall, there wasn't quite as much yard work, and he wasn't coming as often. And why hadn't he called? He'd been embarrassed at the restaurant, so that meant he *knew* he'd hurt her and made her angry. If he cared about her at all, wouldn't he have called?

She tried to keep her spirits up at home. No point in dragging around like her best friend had died. She wasn't about to confide in Paige how depressed she was, and Tuck wouldn't want to hear her troubles, either. He had enough of his own, with Jennifer Bailey still dating Ed Thomas.

"Well," Katie announced cheerfully at the table on the third night, "at least I won't forget Dad's rule about being here for dinner." She managed a weak grin as she speared a pork chop. "I wouldn't want to pick up any bad habits while they're gone."

Tuck laughed. He was in a good mood. In spite of what Katie had just been thinking, Jennifer Bailey had agreed to meet him at the library after dinner so they could work together on the English papers they'd been assigned. She *hadn't* dumped Ed Thomas yet, but she hadn't told Tuck she wouldn't see him, either. Where there's life, Miss Aggie liked to say, there's hope. And until Jennifer Bailey tossed her red hair at him and flashed her brown eyes and said, "Bye-bye, Tuck," he'd hang in there.

Each of the older girls had plans for the evening. Katie Summer was going to grab the bathroom before Paige got in there and wreaked destruction on it. It had been a rough day, and a nice long shower and shampoo were definitely in order. Then a game or two of checkers with Mary Emily and Megan and then some reading for history class. Not an evening to hyperventilate over, but it could be worse. She could, like Tuck, have an English paper to write.

Paige intended to corner Megan in her room after dinner and find out why the long face. And Ben had said he might stop by later and take her for ice cream. She wasn't especially hungry for ice cream. The real treat would be spending even a little time with Ben away from the newspaper office. She glanced over at her younger sister. Megan wasn't eating. Again. She had created a lumpy mountain with her mashed potatoes and was topping it off with her bright green peas. She sat, pale and listless, paying no attention to the conversation flowing around her.

Paige frowned. She had expected Megan to miss their parents, especially her father. Since their mother's death when Megan was only two years old, he had rarely left his daughters overnight. Paige could only guess at how many professional opportunities that had cost him. But he had apparently thought his absence would be too frightening to two young girls who had lost their mother. Looking at Megan now, Paige wondered if it still *was* frightening, at least for one of them. Well, she would find out tonight, and do what she could to put Megan's mind at rest.

They were just getting up to take their plates into the kitchen, when there was a loud crash, followed by a cry, a resounding thud, and then a low moaning sound. They all stood stock-still around the table, plates in hand.

"Miss Aggie!" Paige cried. They put their plates back onto the table and rushed into the kitchen.

CHAPTER 7

Miss Aggie was lying on the white tile, her round face twisted in pain. She was flanked on one side by an overturned kitchen stool, on the other by a seldom-used casserole. Paige knew its usual place was on the top cupboard shelf, and had no trouble figuring out what had just happened.

"Oh, Miss Aggie," she cried, rushing to kneel by the housekeeper's side, "are you all right?"

"Stop looking at me like I was lyin' in my coffin," Miss Aggie commanded, "and help me up." Her voice sounded as strong as ever, and Paige breathed a sigh of relief, as did Katie and Tuck.

But as the three of them helped her to her feet, she grimaced with pain and couldn't repress another moan. She had to lean heavily on Tuck for support. "Oh," she said softly, "it's my back. I've gone and thrown my back out. I've done it before. Just get me home and I'll call my doctor."

"Oh, children," Miss Aggie said as they helped her to a kitchen chair. She sank into it gratefully, biting down hard on her lower lip. "Oh, children, this is terrible. The last time I did this, taking a tumble down those treacherous cellar stairs of mine, I was flat on my back for a week."

"Flat on your back?" Paige asked weakly. "For a week?" Her eyes met Tuck's. They said silently, This is a catastrophe. What do we do now?

Tuck remained calm. "C'mon, Miss Aggie, we'd better get you home. Then you can call your doctor. And your niece lives with you, doesn't she? So you won't be alone?"

Miss Aggie nodded. It was obvious as she hobbled, with Tuck's help, across the floor that she could hardly stand to move one leg after the other. She stopped at the front door and turned to face the worried group. "Will you call your parents or shall I?" she asked.

"Call our parents?" Tuck echoed. "You mean. . . . "

"I mean to tell them to come home, of course. You can't stay here by yourselves. I wouldn't hear of it. They may want Katie's grandmother to come and stay with you. You can find that out from them."

Paige drew in her breath sharply. Another Guthrie in the house? Not if *she* had anything to say about it.

But Katie shook her head. "Don't be silly, Miss Aggie. We wouldn't dream of spoiling Mom and Dad's honeymoon. We'll manage just fine by ourselves. My goodness, we're not ten years old."

"*I* am," Mary Emily piped up. Tuck shushed her with a dirty look.

"Oh, no," Miss Aggie argued. "You *must* call your parents. They think you have an adult here to help you out. They'll be very upset if they come home and find out I wasn't here."

"No, they won't," Tuck said calmly. "Look, you're not here at night, anyway, right? It's not like they were afraid to leave us alone at night. They just wanted someone here to help us with the cleaning and the cooking. And we can do that ourselves. Right, girls?"

"Right!" they said in one enthusiastic voice, although the look on Paige's face showed a definite lack of conviction. But no amount of housework could be worse than having Katie's grandmother move in on them. She was a nice enough lady, but she was even more southern than the Guthries who were already here. Having her around could easily start another Civil War.

"Look, Miss Aggie," Tuck pressed on, "Bill put me in charge, didn't he? So he must have thought I could handle things. If *he* could trust me, you can, too, can't you?"

She's weakening, Katie thought with certainty, seeing the expression of doubt on Miss Aggie's face. She doesn't want to call our folks home any more than we do.

"Miss Aggie," Katie pleaded, "just give us a little time, okay? We'll keep in touch with you by phone and if your back isn't better in a day or two and we're in a real mess here, we can call them then. Fair enough?"

While Miss Aggie thought that over, Tuck

slipped her coat around her shoulders and gestured to Katie to pick up the housekeeper's handbag.

"Well," the housekeeper began, "I suppose — "

"Great!" Tuck interrupted, "I knew you'd see it our way." With great sincerity in his voice, he added, "It just makes sense, Miss Aggie. And you know how Mom approves of us using our common sense." Turning to Katie Summer, he said, "You come with me. Paige, you stay here with the younger girls. The three of you can tackle the kitchen and dining room."

Paige nodded. "You take care now, Miss Aggie," she called as the woman gingerly began to descend the steps with Tuck's help. She was wincing in pain with every movement. "Don't worry about a thing. We'll be fine."

But as she turned away from the door, closing it behind her, she couldn't help wondering if they were biting off more than they could chew. What did they really know about running a household of five people? Six days could be an awfully long time. Too long, certainly, to go without food, for instance. She hoped as she headed for the kitchen, the two younger girls in tow, that the Guthries knew something about cooking. Because Paige Whitman certainly didn't! And she had neither the time nor the inclination to learn now.

Well, first things first, she told herself cheerfully. "C'mon, you two, let's get this place cleaned up. And we'd better save any leftovers because they may be the only thing between us and starvation."

Megan looked up, alarmed. "Are we really going to starve?" she asked, her arms full of dishes.

Paige laughed. "No, honey, we won't starve. Philadelphia is just chock-full of hamburgers, pizza, and Chinese food. And Dad left us plenty of money. So get that frown off your face and help me hunt for the detergent. It must be here somewhere."

By the time Paige had loaded the dishwasher, Mary Emily had unearthed from under the kitchen sink a plastic bottle of dishwashing detergent. Paige poured some into each dishwasher cup and latched the door shut, dialing WASH.

"What about all of *those* dishes?" Mary Emily asked, pointing to a countertop piled high with pots and pans.

"They won't fit. We'll do another load later."

Mary Emily looked doubtful. "Miss Aggie does the pots and pans in the sink. She says Mommy doesn't *like* a messy kitchen."

Paige shrugged. "Well, Mommy's not here," she reminded Mary Emily. "We can just do a second load later, okay?"

"I guess so. But we didn't wipe off the table, either. Megan left crumbs from her dinner roll. She didn't even eat it. She just pulled it to pieces and left a big mess."

"We'll get it later," Paige said absentmindedly, turning off the kitchen light and ushering both girls into the living room. She was trying to remember what she had intended to do this evening. Oh, yes. Talk to Megan. Find out why she wasn't eating and why she was so gloomy. Well, that discussion would have to wait. There wasn't anyone else in the house to distract Mary Emily. Anyway, this current crisis with Miss Aggie was taking up all of her mental energy. She'd talk to Megan tomorrow night.

She was just about to head for the telephone to fill Judy in on the evening's events when the doorbell rang. Answering it, she found Jake standing on the front porch.

"Well," she said, frost edging her words, "look who's honoring the Whitman house with his presence." A bit harsh, maybe, considering how much she'd always liked him. But, in spite of herself, she couldn't forget the look on Katie's face in the restaurant.

Jake's ruddy complexion flushed a deeper shade of red. "Is Katie here?" he asked, standing very stiff and straight.

No wonder Katie is crazy about him, Paige allowed herself to think. As always, he was neatly dressed. In navy corduroy slacks and a pale-blue turtleneck sweater, he looked as if he belonged on a magazine cover, just as Katie so often did. Whether Jake knows it or not, she thought, they're two of a kind.

"No, she's not. And you can't come in and wait for her, because I'm sure she told you we're not allowed to have guests just now."

Before Jake could answer, Tuck and Katie drove up the steep driveway. Katie jumped out of the car and ran toward the porch. Then she saw Jake, and her steps slowed. She hesitated, and then seemed to make up her mind, striding purposefully toward the porch.

But before she could say anything to Jake or Paige, a shout sounded from inside the house. "Paige, Paige!" Mary Emily cried, running to the door to grab Paige's arm, "there are bubbles everywhere! Come quick!" She turned and ran back toward the kitchen, followed closely by Paige, Tuck, Katie, and Jake.

Mary Emily had been exaggerating only slightly. There did indeed seem to be bubbles everywhere in the immediate vicinity of the dishwasher. A lake of bubbly water covered that part of the white tile floor, and a thick froth almost hid the door.

"Oh, no!" Paige wailed, rushing over to release the catch and yank open the door. A wall of bubbles hid the contents from view. "What on earth?"

Katie joined her in her bubbly corner. "Paige, how much detergent did you put in here?"

Paige straightened up, her fair cheeks flaming. "I *know* how much detergent this machine takes. I've lived with it for a long time, remember?"

"Well, you *must* have overloaded it or we wouldn't be looking at this mess!"

Paige was furious. How dare Katie imply that she was stupid, with Jake and Tuck standing right there? "I *put* the right amount in!"

"Well, what did you use, then?"

In a flash of temper, Paige bent and yanked open the cupboard door under the sink. Reaching in, she grabbed the bottle of detergent and thrust it under Katie's nose. "There! See that? It says 'Detergent,' doesn't it?"

"Paige," Katie wailed, "you never, ever put this stuff in the machine! It's for washing dishes by

hand. Miss Aggie uses it on the pots and pans."
Then she spotted the pile of pans on the counter
and said in a disgusted voice, "Which I see you
didn't even bother with."

An embarrassed silence mixed with the sound
of hissing bubbles.

"Oh." That was all Paige could manage to say.
She had never felt so stupid in her life. Of course
she knew that the detergent they used for the
dishwasher came in a box. She'd used it before.
But she'd been distracted by Miss Aggie's accident and then Mary Emily had handed her the
plastic bottle.

In a desperate attempt to defend herself, she
said lamely, "Well, dishwasher detergent *does*
come in a bottle now. I've seen it advertised. I just
assumed Miss Aggie had changed brands."

"Well, never mind," Katie said in a low voice.
"Let's just get this mess cleaned up. We're not
exactly starting off on the right foot, here."

That was true enough, Paige thought dismally.
And there was Jake, standing just a few feet
away, taking in her humiliation with dark eyes.
"He's not supposed to be in here," she snapped.
"You're not supposed to be in here," she shouted
at him. Why didn't he just go away? Why didn't
they *all* go away? She'd clean up her own mess!

"Look," Tuck said patiently, "anybody got any
idea about how to begin getting rid of all these
bubbles?"

Paige saw an opportunity to redeem herself.
"We'll have to take the racks out, with the dishes
still in them. We can set them on the counter.
Then we'll need to scoop out all the bubbles and

the soapy water in the dishwasher until it's empty. We can dump the water down the sink. When it's empty, we'll put the racks back in and put the machine on the rinse cycle."

"How do you know the racks are removable?" Tuck wanted to know. She saw the skepticism in his eyes. She couldn't blame him. After looking at this mess, why would anyone trust her judgment?

"Measuring spoons sometimes get stuck in the back," she explained. "Miss Aggie takes the bottom rack out so she can get at them. I've seen her do it."

That seemed to satisfy Tuck, and he moved forward to follow her suggestion. It worked perfectly. And when Jake moved to help them, no one stopped him. As angry as Katie still was with him, she was grateful for the help. Using large plastic cups, they bent, scooped bubbles and water from the dishwasher, and slopped it into the sink, until the machine was empty of water and suds. Then Jake and Tuck replaced the racks, Katie closed it, and Paige twisted the dial to Rinse.

"There!" she said, "that should do it." But she made no move to leave the machine and stood watching it nervously for several minutes in silence, until it became clear that bubbles weren't about to ooze forth.

"Paige," Katie said quietly, "could I see you in the dining room for a second?"

They left the boys attacking the refrigerator in the kitchen for cold drinks. When they were standing in the dining room, where Katie's eyes quickly surveyed the crumb-laden table before focusing on Paige's guilty expression, she said quietly, "Paige, we have to do better than this. Is *this* the way Miss Aggie leaves the kitchen and dining room after a meal?"

Paige couldn't stand the tone of her stepsister's voice. She sounded so much like Virginia Mae. But she is *not* my mother, she thought angrily, and she's *not* going to talk to me as if she is!

"Oh, Katie, relax," she said, tossing her head with what she hoped was insolence. "Who's going to see it? A few bubbles, a few crumbs, what's the difference? I was too rattled about what happened to Miss Aggie to do a good job." That was sort of true. "How is she, anyway?"

Katie sighed, but allowed the change of subject because she knew she needed to deal with the problem of Jake. Besides, Paige was hopeless. "She's in a lot of pain. I hate seeing her that way. Her niece was calling the doctor when we left. But I honestly don't think Miss Aggie will be back for a while. We're all going to have to sit down and figure out what to do about that. But first," she said, turning to leave the room, "I have to take care of something. I'll be on the front porch for a few minutes."

And it *was* just a few minutes. She wasn't about to get involved in another of those stupid arguments with Jake Carson. Not tonight. Not when she had so much else on her mind. She hadn't invited him here, after all, had she? If she'd wanted to talk to him, she would have called him.

When he turned to her on the front porch and started to speak, she held her hands up in front of her to stop him. "I don't want to talk about it now," she said firmly. She was tired, and she leaned against the wall, wiping a hand across her eyes as if to clear her vision. "Thanks for helping with the mess. We all appreciate it. But you have to go home now." Or wherever, she thought bitterly. Maybe Sandra what's-her-name is free tonight. I'll bet she certainly isn't amusing herself with a bubbling dishwasher.

"I made that date before I saw you the other night," Jake said quietly, wishing she would at least look at him instead of staring at the porch floor that way. "It was something my father suggested, and it didn't seem like such a bad idea at the time. I was sorry the minute I walked into the restaurant and saw you sitting there."

Katie knew that if they really got into this discussion, she was going to cry in front of him, because she was tired, because she was upset with the situation at home, and because he had really hurt her.

"Jake," she said clearly, looking at him then, "I have to go inside. We've got a lot of things to figure out. And I just can't think about this business with you right now. It'll have to wait."

And, leaving him standing there, she turned and went inside, closing the door firmly after her. And locking it.

When he heard the key turn, he gave up. Shoulders slumped, he left, shaking his head grimly.

Katie watched from behind the lace curtain, tears gathering in her eyes, as Jake left the porch and disappeared down the hill.

Then she turned around and called wearily, "Tuck! We need a family meeting!"

CHAPTER 8

Look, it's no big deal," Katie Summer insisted when they were all seated around the dining room table, free now of crumbs. "I did a lot of the housework in Atlanta. It's mostly, just like Miss Aggie says, a matter of organization."

Tuck looked relieved.

Paige looked anything but. Oh, no, she was thinking as she toyed with her blue place mat, now Suzy Homemaker is going to start issuing commands, like a guard at a maximum security prison. I can hear it now: dust this, polish that, clean *this*, clean *that*. She'll probably expect me to dust the Venetian blinds with a toothbrush and color-code all the sheets! Paige had no intention of taking orders from her younger stepsister. It was bad enough that she had to share one room with a person who actually hung up every article of clothing she took off. Now she'd be sharing the whole *house* with her!

"I'll cook when I can," Katie went on, "but I get home so late from swim practice, it'll have to be simple things. Sandwiches, omelettes, things like that. I hope that's okay with everyone."

And she'll serve lots of bunny food, too, I'll bet, Paige thought grimly. She'll probably feed us so many carrot sticks, our skin will turn orange. Still, at least she hadn't asked Paige to cook.

"Paige, you'll have to cook sometimes, too."

Paige stared.

Tuck hooted. "She doesn't know how to do *dishes*, and you're going to put our lives and health in her hands? Are you crazy?"

Paige lashed out in an attempt at self-defense, "Anyone could have made a mistake with the detergent! What does that have to do with cooking? I've cooked more than once for my father." That was true. No need to discuss the results of her efforts: burned pizza crust, soup boiled almost beyond recognition, hot dogs blasted to smithereens in the microwave. Past culinary errors didn't count. If Katie could do it, she could, too. Nothing to it.

"There's always fast food," Tuck offered. "It won't kill us, and Bill gave me money in case we needed it. And I can cook, too."

Katie laughed. "You're a worse cook than Paige."

Paige nodded gratefully, ignoring Katie's remark. "Fast food makes sense, don't you think, Katie? Our schedules are pretty hectic already. If Megan and Mary Emily have to wait for us to get home and fix a meal, they're going to get awfully pale and wan from hunger." She liked

69

the way she sounded: reasonable and mature and extremely cooperative.

But Katie wasn't about to shout Bravo! "Well, I guess it couldn't hurt for a day or two," she said, sounding unconvinced. She didn't approve of fast foods and had said so many times. "At least until we're sure we have things under control. But," she added firmly, sounding very like Virginia Mae again, "then we'll have to make sure we all eat properly. Now, let's see about dividing the housework. I guess we should have made those lists when Tuck first suggested it. Well, we'll just do it now."

"*I'll* make the lists," Tuck said. "Bill left me in charge. Besides," he added with a sardonic grin, "if you two start haggling over who's going to do what, we'll be here all night. And I'm tired. You can't argue with me, because I'm the boss."

He tried to be fair, dividing up the necessary tasks as equally as possible. Although Paige moaned and made some interesting faces as she read the list he handed her, she didn't complain. Nor did Katie.

But when they got to their room, Katie cheerfully pinned her list to the ribbon hung with souvenirs over her bed, so that it would be in full view. Paige, on the other hand, dropped hers carelessly into the sea of clutter hiding her half of their dresser.

Watching her, Katie Summer thought, Oh-oh. She's not taking any of this seriously. I am *not* going to get stuck with more than my share. I don't have time for that. But, glancing in dismay at Paige's chaotic half of the room, she wondered how she could expect much housekeeping help from a person whose idea of making a bed was simply removing herself from the bedding.

Katie Summer went to sleep hoping for a miracle that would turn her stepsister Paige into a reasonable facsimile of a neat person.

She didn't get her miracle. It soon became obvious that on Paige's list of life's priorities, good housekeeping ranked somewhere between studying the life cycle of the tsetse fly and dyeing her hair green. She simply saw no sense in the rule Miss Aggie had drummed into her: "a place for everything and everything in its place."

"I just don't understand," she complained early on the first morning of their new schedule, "why people make beds. We're just going to crawl back into them at night. What a colossal waste of time!"

Katie managed, with great effort, to remain silent. But that wasn't the end of it. They had settled on cold cereal with hot toast and orange juice as the fastest, easiest breakfast. With Paige doing her part, the meal became cold cereal and cold toast. And she was the only member of the family who failed to take her dishes to the sink and rinse them. Saying she had to meet Ben at the newspaper office before her first class, she dashed away, leaving the kitchen cleanup for the others.

Katie and Tuck exchanged annoyed glances.

"I'll do Paige's stuff," Megan volunteered. "It's not that much, anyway." She didn't want anyone angry with her older sister.

"Okay," Tuck said, "you can this morning, be-

71

cause we're late. But tonight I'll make it clear to her that she has to pull her own weight from now on. She'll just have to postpone any early morning meetings. I don't care *who* they're with."

But Paige cared, and although she did feel a pang or two of guilt for running out on kitchen duty, she hadn't lied about the meeting with Ben. He had an idea for a feature series that he wanted to discuss with her. She was flattered that he cared what she thought. Dirty dishes couldn't be more important than *that*.

What shocked her out of her shoes was that Ben thought they might be. She made the mistake of explaining the situation at home to him, adding that she had hurried to make this meeting with him.

"You mean you just walked out?"

They were in the newspaper office, unusually quiet with just the two of them there.

"It was just a few cereal bowls, Ben, not the remains of a twelve-course meal."

"That's not the point. You said you all agreed to share the work load. Just like we do on the paper. I don't see you as a shirker, Paige."

That really stung. It wouldn't have, had it come from Katie or Tuck. But there were a dozen ways in which she wanted Ben to see her and "shirker" definitely wasn't one of them.

"I'll take care of it tonight," she protested. "No one's going to take a tour of our house today, so what's the difference? All we had for breakfast was cereal, anyway." She saw no point in mentioning toast that was as black as coal and as cold as snow.

Ben's thin face contorted in a look of disgust. "Yuck! Nothing's worse than cereal bowls with dried-out flakes cemented to their sides. You need a potent paint remover to get that stuff off."

Paige laughed. "I didn't realize you were such an expert on dirty dishes."

"I've done my share of dishes." He took her elbow to lead her from the office. "I," he said, "unlike certain other people whose name I shall not mention, have acquainted myself quite well with the appliance known as the automatic dishwasher."

She laughed again. "You sound like the butler in a Victorian novel."

He shook his head. "They didn't have dishwashers in Victorian novels."

"Okay, okay," Paige said, shaking her head, "I give up. You're right, I did goof up this morning. I promise I'll try harder tonight. Now can we get off the subject of my failure at domesticity? Tell me about your new idea."

Ben explained his new idea to her as they walked. Half listening, Paige told herself that she would make more of an effort at home. She had promised her father, after all, and that was *before* Miss Aggie took her fall.

She paid attention, then, and made several comments about Ben's new features idea. It was a series on job hunting after graduation, and she thought it would be valuable to the students and said so.

"Okay, what about Friday night?" he asked as they reached her first period class.

She grinned. "What about it?"

73

"Want to see a movie?"

Virginia Mae hadn't said they couldn't go out. She had only said other people couldn't come into the house. "Sure. Love to."

"Great. See you later."

She watched him go, shoulders hunched as always, long legs carrying him quickly down the hall. She noticed that people greeted him as he went, and the lucky ones got a brusque nod or a casual wave of the hand. Most got no response at all, but didn't seem offended. Everyone who knew Ben understood that he wasn't Mr. Personality, but forgave him for it because they trusted and respected him. Editor of the newspaper was a prestige job. You didn't get it, Paige reflected as she took her place in class, by being charming. You got it by proving that you knew what you were doing. And Ben had proved that. She loved that about him. In fact, she thought happily as she waved at Judy, I love almost everything about him. But she frowned as she opened her textbook. Everything, that is, except his atrocious habit of lecturing me when he thinks I'm wrong. Which happens a lot more than I think it should.

But remembering the mess she'd left with Tuck and Katie, she realized Ben had been right this time.

To her relief, Tuck decided on fast food for the first two nights. The only cleaning up they needed to do was toss the empty bags and napkins and paper cups into the trash bin. The house still bore the signs of Miss Aggie's efficiency and needed little in the way of heavy-duty elbow grease. Still, there were things that needed to be done.

"Who wears all these clothes?" Paige wanted to know as she brought a basketful up from the basement early in the evening.

"We all do," Katie answered calmly. She was wiping off the kitchen counters, a task Paige regarded skeptically as being totally unnecessary. They hadn't even *cooked*! "And we all use the towels and washcloths and — "

"Never mind," Paige snapped, setting the basket on the little round table in one corner of the kitchen. "You don't have to draw me a picture." She got busy folding the clothes. No one could say she hadn't been doing her part. She had to admit (silently) that Katie always seemed appreciative. Or maybe that was just surprise that brought forth a "thanks, Paige." She probably thought I'd be a total washout at this domestic stuff, Paige thought with a grin as she folded Megan's jeans. And I'm not doing such a rotten job. It must kill her to find out she's not the only person in this house who knows how to run a vacuum or whip a dust cloth across a desk.

Not that Paige had done any of those things yet. But she decided she would when the need arose. And she'd do them well, too. Or die trying.

Thursday evening, the two younger girls complained to Tuck that they were hungry for "real" food. "Okay, no problem," he said, thinking to himself that since he rushed home from school each afternoon to keep an eye on Megan and Mary Emily, the least Katie Summer or Paige could do was cook a decent meal.

Paige arrived home first, and Tuck agreed with her that they should wait for Katie, since she had the most kitchen experience. But when five-thirty came and Katie still hadn't arrived, Tuck came into the kitchen, where Paige was studying, and suggested that she at least begin the meal.

"You can get things started, can't you?" he asked as she looked startled.

"I can set the table, I guess. But I thought that was Megan's job."

"No," he said impatiently, "I don't mean doing stuff like that. Can't you start cooking something so we can eat at six-thirty? If we wait for Katie, we'll be dying of hunger pains before the food is on the table."

Paige knew he was right. And she imagined Ben's hazel eyes on her face, his voice saying earnestly, "C'mon, Paige, your family needs you. You can do it, and you *should*."

"Okay, Tuck, I'll give it a whirl," she said, getting up and closing her book and notebook. "But I don't want anyone looking over my shoulder, so you go in the living room with Megan and Mary Emily, while I whip us up something fantastic. *You* wouldn't be a help here, now. You can clean up."

He grinned and left. The kitchen was all hers.

The question is, she thought, heading for the cookbook shelf above the microwave stand, what do I *do* with the kitchen now that I've got it?

CHAPTER 9

Paige Whiteman was one of the most intelligent girls at Harrison High school. She was perfectly capable of reading and executing a recipe. Deciding that if she was going to do this she might as well do it right, she selected a recipe of Miss Aggie's that she knew everyone liked. She read it aloud. It sounded fast and simple, which was exactly what she wanted. Checking first to make sure the necessary ingredients were on hand, she went to work. Preparation of that casserole seemed to go so well that with it in the oven, she decided to branch out and create a dessert. She settled on vanilla pudding after locating two boxes of pudding mix in the pantry.

Humming softly to herself, she swept aside the litter of pots and pans left on the stove-top by her casserole preparation and mixed the contents of both packages with the proper amount of milk in one of the few remaining clean saucepans. Megan and Mary Emily loved vanilla pudding. She would put a maraschino cherry on each of their servings as an added treat. That might make even Megan smile. And for once, they'd all be smiling because of something *she* had done, not something Katie Summer had done.

This was fun. If she'd known it would be so easy, she'd have tried sooner. Maybe when Miss Aggie came back, she'd surprise her by cooking a meal or two. And wouldn't her parents just be knocked out of their socks if they sat down to a scrumptious meal prepared by the daughter who didn't know her way around a kitchen?

Tuck poked his head around a corner just once. He surveyed the kitchen, which Paige had to admit looked like the site of an archeological dig, saying only, "Wow! When did the bomb land?"

"Never mind," Paige responded cheerfully. "Wait'll you taste dinner. You're all in for a real treat. And nothing good comes without effort," she added loftily, "you just remember that."

Skepticism written all over his face, he disappeared.

Paige needed to share her adventure with someone. With the casserole safely in the oven and the pudding boiling happily away on the stove, why not call Judy? It might be nice to report for a change that *she*, not Katie, was in charge. Even if it was only temporary.

Judy's singular lack of enthusiasm for Paige's kitchen accomplishments didn't prevent them from carrying on a twenty-minute long conversation. It might have stretched out indefinitely if

Megan hadn't caught Paige's attention by calling, "Paige! What's that awful smell?"

Paige whirled to face the stove. "Oh, my gosh!" Her beautiful pudding had escaped the confines of its too-small container and was covering the stove surface with thick rivulets of creamy liquid. "Oh, no! Gotta go, Judy, 'bye!" Paige slammed down the receiver and dashed to the stove. In her urgency to stop the spreading pudding pool, she grabbed the pan's handle without a potholder. The pain was instant and fierce. Crying out, she let go, slopping more of the hot pudding across the floor and onto the tops of her boots.

And at that precise moment, Katie's voice split the air with a maddening inquiry: "Oh, my goodness! What *is* that horrid smell?"

Paige, her back to Katie, groaned silently as she swabbed frantically at the gooey mess, using a kitchen towel that would never be the same. Talk about timing! Pasting a cheerful smile on her face, she switched her wiping motions from frantic to casual. "Oh, hi, Katie. I guess I burned this pudding. Judy called with a minor emergency, you know how *that* goes and — "

"No," Katie said, joining Paige at the stove. "It's not the pudding that I smell." She tilted the pan toward Paige. "See? It boiled over, but it's *not* burned. Something else is burning."

Paige closed her eyes. No, she thought, no, no, *no*! There was only one something else cooking. Only one something else available for burning. Her casserole. Without it, dinner was nonexistent. She didn't think she could bear that.

But looking down, she saw little curls of smoke

edging the oven door. Wishing with all her heart that Katie would magically disappear, Paige gingerly pulled open the oven door. Let it be all right, she thought, painfully conscious of Katie standing beside her.

The casserole was definitely not "all right." Burned dark enough to be virtually unrecognizable, it stared sadly at Paige. She wondered for one crazy moment if someone had played a cruel trick on her. Had Mary Emily or Megan thought it would be hilarious to sneak in here and replace her gorgeous casserole with this hideous blackened mess?

"No wonder it's burned," Katie said as Paige surveyed the contents of the oven in dismay. "You've set the oven dial at five hundred and fifty degrees instead of three hundred and fifty. Goodness, Paige, the only thing you use such a high temperature for is broiling. It's too hot for anything else."

Her tone of voice maddened Paige. Arming herself with potholders, she said, "Excuse me while I remove the corpse. I guess I read the recipe wrong. I was sure it said five hundred and fifty degrees." With the casserole safely on the pudding-puddled stove, she stared at it in silent despair as the rest of the family arrived to inquire about the status of their dinner.

"It's ruined," Paige admitted softly, "it's absolutely ruined."

Megan and Mary Emily groaned. "Aren't we going to get any dinner?" Mary Emily asked Katie. While Megan muttered, "I wish Mother was here!" And Tuck added sourly, "I guess it's fast-food again tonight. I should have known."

"No," Katie told them, "it's okay." She could see that Paige was fighting back tears. She wanted to sympathize, but the truth was, she was really tired, and a little depressed, herself. It had been a long, hard day, with Jake on her mind during most of it. She had intended to come home, eat, and then soak in a hot tub to take her mind off her troubles. The last thing in the world she felt like doing was cooking a meal. But she knew what Miss Aggie and their parents would say if they ate fast-food hamburgers three nights in a row. "I'll just whip us up some scrambled eggs. They're really good cooked in the microwave. And we'll have English muffins and applesauce. And cookies and ice cream for dessert. How does that sound?"

"That sounds fine," Tuck said, his eyes on Paige, his voice grim. "What can we do to help?"

"You can do the muffins. Megan and Mary Emily can set the table. We'll be eating in no time, I promise."

"I really thought the recipe said five hundred and fifty degrees," Paige said in a dull voice. She wanted, needed, someone to say, "Gee, that's okay, Paige, anyone could have made a little mistake like that," or, "Well, no wonder! Who can read Miss Aggie's handwriting?"

No one said anything like that. Megan said instead, "But I wanted pudding! Paige, you said — "

"Never mind what I said!" Paige snapped.

"And don't whine! You're too big to be whining!" She was sorry immediately, but Megan had already whirled and run out of the room. Mary Emily threw Paige an accusing look before following Megan.

"Nice going, Paige," Tuck commented. Shaking his head in disgust, he took a package of English muffins from the refrigerator while Katie busied herself with the egg carton and a bowl.

It's happening again, Paige thought as she half-heartedly mopped at rapidly congealing pudding. Everything was going so well and now, just because of this one tiny little mistake, everyone hates me again. And Katie's scrambled eggs will be delicious and she'll be a heroine again. She should write a book. She could call it *Katie Saves the Day*. Paige got down on her hands and knees and began scrubbing the white tile. And it'll sell a million copies, and she'll become rich and famous while I'm still trying to figure out how to put a decent meal on the table!

When Katie called, "Okay, everybody, soup's on!" Paige was strongly tempted to say casually, "Oh, gee, I'm just not the least bit hungry. Thanks, anyway." Such a statement would have given her ego enormous satisfaction. Unfortunately, it wouldn't have done a thing for the hunger pangs that were making her knees weak. She could either swallow her pride *and* Katie's eggs or head for the peanut butter jar. The eggs looked delicious: light and fluffy and exactly the right shade of pale yellow. Just the way Paige liked them.

"I'll bring the milk," she said. Her ego would

just have to wait for satisfaction. Tonight her stomach came first.

She even managed, in a roundabout way, to compliment Katie on the meal. All she actually said was "Um-hmmm" when Mary Emily said, "These eggs are the best, Katie Summer!" but considering her depressed state of mind, she felt that the "Um-hmmm" was worth quite a lot. Then Tuck twisted the knife by commenting around a mouthful of scrambled egg, "It's a good thing *some*one around here can cook!" and Paige retreated into angry silence for the remainder of the meal.

The younger girls had kitchen duty that night. But Paige knew there was no way she could expect them to clean up her mess. While Katie called Miss Aggie's house to find out how the housekeeper was feeling, Paige trudged into the kitchen, her face grim, and picked up a sponge. The sink was occupied by several pans soaking in soapy water. Katie's doing, no doubt, Paige thought as she noticed the pans *she* had used, coated with hardened food. She'd be lucky if she got them clean before her nineteenth birthday! Why hadn't she thought to soak them? Katie would be through in the kitchen long before she was.

Katie was. But after putting the last of her clean dishes away, she turned to Paige and asked, "Need some help?" She had already helped Megan and Mary Emily, who had finished their chores and gone upstairs.

Annoyed with herself, Paige chose to take out her annoyance on her more efficient stepsister.

"No, thank you very much," she said crisply. "I prefer to clean up my own messes."

Katie laughed. "Oh, Paige," she said, "you don't prefer any such thing! No one can stand to go into the bathroom after you've been in there, because they're afraid of what they'll find."

Paige continued doggedly to scrub at a thick blob of vanilla pudding. "Well, I'm turning over a new leaf. Go paint your toenails or something."

"Honestly, Paige, you are *so* rude! I was just trying to be helpful. My mother should forget about Tuck and Mary Emily and me and concentrate on *your* manners for about a hundred years!" And she turned on her heel and ran out of the kitchen, leaving Paige still on her hands and knees.

By the time Paige had finally finished, the house was quiet, the first floor emptied of all but her and Binker, stretched out on a small braided rug just inside the front door. "They're not coming home tonight, cat," Paige said as she began climbing the stairs. "I guess you can't read a calendar, hmm?" She was so tired every muscle in her body was begging her to lie down. A hot bath would do more good than a shower. But why did she have the nagging feeling that she'd forgotten something?

She was already in the bathroom, bubble bath in hand, when she remembered: she had planned to talk to Megan. Well, she was too tired tonight. Her brain was so fuzzed up from this rotten day, her words would probably come out backward or upside down.

But Megan hadn't eaten much at dinner. Even

Katie's eggs hadn't tempted her. She'd pushed them around on her plate with her fork, and her milk had remained in its glass throughout the meal. If the honeymooners came home and found Megan pale and unhappy, wouldn't they blame her older sister?

She sighed and headed for Megan's room. On the way there, she heard voices coming from the room she shared with Katie. Good. That meant Mary Emily was probably in there with her. Maybe Megan was, too, but she hadn't seemed in the mood for chatter.

Megan was lying across her bed, the lights out, holding a stuffed Panda close to her chest. Paige flipped on a small table lamp beside the bed and sat down beside Megan.

"Honey, I'm sorry I snapped at you," she began. "I felt terrible about the casserole burning, and I guess I wasn't in a very good mood. I'm sorry."

Megan rolled over and looked up at her. "That's okay, Paige," she said quietly. "I guess I was whining."

"No, you weren't. I'm sorry about the pudding, too." She laughed. "I think it'll be a while before I try my hand at cooking again."

"Well," Megan said loyally, "I'm sure the pudding would have been really good if it hadn't spilled."

"It didn't 'spill,' Megan," Paige said with a grin. "It boiled over. There's a difference."

Paige liked the way the two younger girls had decorated their room, and with no arguing at all. Megan had her movie posters, Mary Emily her horse pictures, and their stuffed animals shared a wall bookcase. It really was nice that they got along so well. Too bad she couldn't say the same for the older stepsisters.

"Listen, Megan," she said seriously, "you're not eating anything at all. And you've been moping around for days now. I'm worried about you. What's the matter?"

"Nothing." But the expression on Megan's face told Paige she wasn't telling the truth.

"C'mon, Meg. You can tell me. Mom and Dad will be mad if they get home and you're like this."

"But I won't *be* like this when they get home!" Megan said, sitting up. Then she turned away, murmuring, "*If* they get home."

Paige heard the murmur. She laughed. "What do you mean, *if* they get home? Of course they'll get home. They just went on a trip. They'll be home next Wednesday."

Megan said nothing.

Paige thought for a minute. "Megan? Megan, are you afraid something is going to happen to Dad and Virginia Mae? Did that silly remark of Tuck's about the volcanoes scare you?"

Megan stiffened, and Paige realized she was zeroing in on the problem. "You *are* scared! Oh, Megan, Tuck was just being funny. Dad wouldn't have taken Virginia Mae to Hawaii if there was anything at all dangerous there. You know that. Nothing bad is going to happen to them, I promise."

Megan looked at her then, her eyes full of tears. "Something happened to Miss Aggie, didn't it? And . . . and something really bad happened to our real mother, didn't it?"

"Oh, Megan." Paige thought suddenly, I'm not up to this. She's really frightened, and I don't know what to say to her. Then, angrily, Why isn't *Dad* here for this? She took a deep breath to calm herself. "Megan, that was a long, long time ago. And our mother didn't go on a trip. She was very, very sick. Dad and Virginia Mae aren't sick, you know that. It's not at all the same thing. You can understand that, can't you?" She knew Megan didn't really remember their mother. She'd been too young, just two, when the death occurred. But of course she'd missed having a mother as she grew up. Why wouldn't she? And she loved Virginia Mae. Paige supposed Megan was thinking that she'd lost one mother, maybe she'd lose another, especially with Virginia Mae going so far away. And that remark of Tuck's probably hadn't helped.

"I know what," Paige said. "We know where Dad and Virginia Mae are. Why don't we call them Saturday afternoon and you can talk to them? Will that help?"

Megan smiled, and Paige breathed a sigh of relief. It had been the right thing to suggest. "You mean it, Paige? It must cost an awful lot of money to call Hawaii. You don't think Daddy will be mad?"

"I think he'll be thrilled to death to talk to you. But *I'm* going to talk to him, too," Paige added, pulling the coverlet back so Megan could slip under it, "and I want to be able to tell him we're all fine and happy. So you'll have to eat really well tomorrow and put some roses in those cheeks so I won't have to fib to him about how you're doing. Okay?"

"Okay! I promise! I can't wait to talk to them!"

Paige tucked her in and turned out the light. "No more worrying, okay?" she said as she went to the door. "You'll hear for yourself just how fine they both are on Saturday. So relax and go to sleep. See you in the morning."

"Paige?"

"Hmm?"

"Don't tell Miss Aggie, but I never really liked that casserole she makes."

In the darkness, Paige smiled. "Night-night, honey. Sleep tight, and don't let the bedbugs bite."

"G'night, Paige."

Soaking in a hot tub a few minutes later, Paige decided it hadn't been such a terrible day, after all. So she was a rotten cook. So what? She'd made her sister smile, hadn't she? That should be worth something.

Lying back in the tub, she began to hum.

CHAPTER 10

If Katie and Tuck noticed the following morning that Paige was unusually attentive to her younger sister, they chose not to comment on it. While Paige packed lunches for the two younger girls, Katie and Tuck put breakfast on the table.

While they were eating, Paige told Tuck, "Don't forget, I have a date tonight. But," she added, "I'll do kitchen duty before I leave."

"You sure will." The shirt Tuck was wearing had a spot just above the pocket. Preoccupied with the dinner problems the night before, no one had thought to do any laundry.

"Tuck," Katie pointed out, "if Mom saw you leaving the house in that, she'd have a fit. Don't you have anything else to wear?"

"Well, she isn't here, is she? And I don't think she's going to waltz in here next Wednesday and ask me if I wore a clean shirt every day. So what difference does it make?"

Tuck just wasn't himself these days, Katie decided as she took her dishes to the sink. Did he resent having to "baby-sit" Megan and Mary Emily every day after school? But he was the logical choice, since he had no extracurricular activities right now. Still, it probably was boring for him. Was that it? Or was he just not getting anywhere with Jennifer? Striking out with her could easily put that sour expression on his face.

"Tuck, I'll be home tonight if you want to go out," Katie offered, anxious to cheer him up. "I'll stay with Megan and Mary Emily."

To her relief, he looked interested. "Maybe I *will* go out and see what's going on in the real world." He started to ask Katie if Jake was coming over as he sometimes did on Friday nights and stopped himself just in time. Mentioning Jake would make Katie look the way *he* felt most of the time lately. No point in both of them being lower than the ocean floor. Although Katie probably felt that way already. She just hid it better than he did.

Megan turned to Paige and asked anxiously, "We're still going to call Hawaii tomorrow, aren't we, Paige?"

Before Tuck or Katie could comment, Paige said firmly, "Yes, we are. So you get busy and think of a whole bunch of good stuff to tell Virginia Mae and Dad. If they thing *we're* having a good time, they'll have a good time, too."

"*I'm* having a good time," Mary Emily cried cheerfully. "So can I talk to Mommy in Hawaii, too?"

Paige laughed. As she stood up, she said, "Yes,

of course you can. But you both have to be careful not to mention Miss Aggie's fall. If they knew she wasn't here with us they'd probably come rushing right home. We'll be ruining their trip if we tell them. Okay? You both promise?"

Megan nodded solemnly and Mary Emily agreed. "We'll just say Miss Aggie is fine, because that's what she told Katie last night on the phone. She said the doctor told her she can come back to work on Monday and she'll be fit as a . . . what was that thing she said, Katie?"

"A fiddle. Fit as a fiddle. Now you two, get your lunches and get going. It's time for school." They obeyed, giggling about a fiddle being fit as they bumped into each other scrambling out of their chairs.

"Paige," Katie said as her stepsister brought her dishes to the sink, "don't forget, curfew is at twelve o'clock."

"Yes, *Mother*," Paige mocked. "Don't worry about it."

Katie flushed. "I wasn't worried. I just — "

"You just like to treat me as if one of my burners didn't have a working pilot light, that's all. You keep forgetting I functioned perfectly well for years before you ever came on the scene."

"No, I — "

"Forget it. See you," Paige said deliberately and stalked out of the kitchen.

She's right, Katie thought sadly as the navy blue sweater disappeared from sight. I'm a perfectionist. I don't mean to be. I don't want people hating me, but I just can't seem to help acting like Mom. No wonder Jake hasn't called. He probably knows that about me and can't stand it.

But then common sense took over, reminding Katie in the next minute that her tendency to play "little mother" had never manifested itself when Jake was around. No, a girl in a red dress was their most recent problem.

At lunch in the school cafeteria, Judy Belnap asked Paige if she was going to the football game that night.

Paige shook her head. "It's an away game. With my folks out of town, we all have to stick close to home. I guess my stepmother thinks it's easier to have a terrible accident when they're out of town."

Deirdre Nichols, a girl in Paige's homeroom, was passing behind Paige and overheard her reply. She stopped in her tracks. "Your folks are away?" she asked in a sultry voice that matched her black leather miniskirt and hot-pink turtleneck. "So when's the party?"

"*No* party," Paige said flatly, not looking up. "And lower your voice, will you? You'll have the entire student body on my front porch in five seconds." She knew Deirdre well enough to know that if ever there was a time for a convincing lie, this was it. "They're coming back tonight. Early." That should keep Deirdre and her friends away.

Deirdre's face sagged with disappointment, which was quickly replaced by skepticism. "Yeah? I thought you said you couldn't go to the game because your folks were away. If they're due back tonight, why can't you go to the game?"

Paige sighed heavily like someone dealing with

a difficult child. "*Because* they're coming home tonight, that's why! They expect all of us to be there for their homecoming. Wouldn't *your* parents?"

Shrug. "Not mine," Deirdre answered airily. "They'd prob'ly be disappointed if I showed up."

"Well," Paige murmured to Judy, "I can certainly understand that!"

Deirdre didn't hear her. She said with disgust, "Nobody ever gives parties in this town! I mean, it's a boring city, know what I mean?" With that, she sauntered off to a table occupied by most of the football team.

"Your folks aren't really coming back tonight, are they?" Judy asked. "I thought you said they were going to be gone for nine days."

"No, they're not coming back tonight. Think she bought it?" she said with a shrug in Deirdre's direction. "I mean, a secret in her possession is about as safe as a mouse in a cat's mouth. I *had* to fib. Or sometime this weekend, all of Harrison High would be using my house to create their own party."

"Well, not tonight. Tonight they'll be at an away game, so you can relax."

Paige shrugged. "I won't be home, anyway. I didn't say I couldn't go *out*, I just said I couldn't go out of town. Ben's taking me to a movie."

Judy grinned in spite of Paige's casual tone of voice. "Oh, yeah? That's two weekends in a row now. Things heating up between you two?"

"It's just a movie, Judy." But Paige couldn't control the grin that lit up her face.

"Yeah, sure. Well, personally, I think you're

made for each other. Ben's a little stiff and prickly but then," she added, "so are you sometimes."

"Judy Belnap! I am as sweet and soft as cotton candy."

"No, no, no, Paige Whitman," Judy said, as they began to gather up their things, "you're very confused. The cotton candy person in your family is your sister *Katie*. You, m'dear, are those little yellow lemon drops."

That stung. "Ju-dee! How can you call your very best friend a sour old lemon drop?"

Judy relented. "I *like* lemon drops. Lots of people do."

They made their way out of the cafeteria. Paige spotted Katie at a front table. She was laughing at something Don Bedford had said, her head thrown back, blue eyes shining. Cotton candy? Paige thought with contempt. Judy must mean her *brain*!

"Anyway," Judy was saying in an attempt to get back on the right footing, "sometimes lemon drops taste a little sweet."

But Paige refused to be mollified. She parted from her best friend with a chilly, "See you." If it hadn't been for her date with Ben that night, she would have been really depressed. Was the way Judy described her and Katie the way everyone saw them? No, it couldn't be. She knew most of her friends didn't like it when she made snide remarks about her stepsister, and she had really made an effort to stop it. Everyone had begun to see her as spiteful and jealous, even unfair, and she couldn't stand that. So she'd tried very hard to keep a tight rein on her tongue. But if Judy still saw her as a "lemon drop," maybe it wasn't working.

Well, she thought angrily as she walked to her next class, I am *not* going to run around this school calling everybody "Sugah." That's just not me. So I'm a lemon drop, so what? Like Judy said, lots of people like lemon drops.

Besides, she told herself as she took her seat, I have never, ever, liked gooey, sticky, disgustingly *pink* cotton candy! Yuk!

Katie spent most of the day worrying about the coming evening meal. It really should be Paige's turn to cook. Fair was fair, after all. But after last night's disaster, suggesting that her step-sister try again seemed sheer folly. If I *don't* suggest it, though, she fretted, she'll know that means I don't think she can do it. And she'll get all prickly and witchy. Or she'll accuse me of thinking I can do everything better than her. And *this* evening will be worse than last night. If that's possible!

Katie was very tired. She was beginning to think they'd made a terrible mistake not telling their parents about Miss Aggie's fall. They'd find out, anyway, when they returned. And unless everything had gone really well without the housekeeper there, they would be angry.

Unless things went really well? Who am I kidding? Katie thought. A snowball in Paige's five hundred-and-fifty degree oven has a better chance of doing well than the five Guthrie and Whitman kids on their own did, at least if you judged by how things have gone so far. If Paige would only get that stupid chip off her shoulder! Like this morning when I had reminded her about curfew. What had been so terrible about that? Paige could have forgotten that we're under strict orders not to break curfew just because Mom and Bill aren't here.

But that isn't why you reminded her, a little voice in her head whispered. You sounded just like some goody two-shoes, and you know it! Like you yourself would never even *think* of breaking curfew. When the truth is, if that stubborn, pig-headed Jake Carson popped by some night, you wouldn't even *glance* at a clock the whole time he was with you. True or not true?

Katie grinned. True, she admitted silently as Don Bradford stood in front of the class attempting to explain nuclear power, very true.

Not, she thought grimly, that there is any chance of Jake Carson honoring me with his presence. I don't even *own* a red dress!

Depressed by her current train of thought, she returned to her dread of the evening meal. She'd get home in time for it, because she had promised. But she wasn't looking forward to it.

To Katie's enormous relief, Tuck had dinner under control when she arrived home just minutes after Paige. The table was set and Tuck was carrying a huge casserole of hot stew to the table. Megan followed close behind with a basket of hot biscuits.

"Stew came out of a can, biscuits did the same," Tuck said cryptically as they sat down to eat. He threw Katie a smile. "I figured, since

96

Paige and I are taking off tonight, you shouldn't have to cook."

"Thanks, Tuck," she said gratefully, returning the smile. His bad mood seemed to have lifted, probably because he was going out. And she knew he was hoping he'd run into Jennifer Bailey. Silently, she wished him luck.

Dinner went well, with the two younger girls chattering about the promised phone call to Hawaii, and Paige and Tuck looking forward to their night out. No one seemed to notice that Katie was uncharacteristically silent, and she was as grateful for that as she was for the already-prepared meal.

Paige cleaned up the kitchen, as promised, and was ready when Ben arrived. Tuck left soon after that, and Katie settled into a quiet evening with the two younger girls. At bedtime, she sent them upstairs, promising a story when 'they were in their pajamas. She was in the process of putting away the games they'd played when the doorbell rang. Surprised, she stood up straight and glanced toward the front door. Maybe Tuck had struck out and come home early, forgetting his key.

She slid the game boxes into their proper places and went to the door. "Honestly, Tuck," she began as she pulled the door open . . . to find Jake Carson standing on her front porch, wearing a suede jacket in a soft buttery tan, khaki slacks, and a tentative smile.

CHAPTER 11

Did you want something?" Katie asked politely, wishing she had done something with her hair, still in its swim practice ponytail.

"Yes. I want to talk to you."

She hated that no-nonsense tone of voice. He always used it when he had every intention of getting what he wanted. "Well, you can't. I told you, we're not allowed to have anyone in while our parents are away."

He shifted from one foot to the other but remained standing firmly upright. Ready to do battle, she thought, repressing a giggle. This really wasn't funny. What was he *doing* here? "I'm not just anybody," he said. "I work here. Your stepfather trusts me. I know he wouldn't mind if I came in. You know it, too, don't you Katie Summer?"

A picture of Jake with the girl in the red dress at his side flashed through Katie's mind. "I don't know any such thing," she said in a cool voice. "He didn't say don't let anyone in but Jake Carson! And it wasn't him, anyway. It was my mother who made that rule. And *she* hardly knows you."

Jake's lips tightened. "You're just using that as an excuse. Why won't you let me explain about Saturday night? Don't you *want* an explanation?"

Hadn't he told her he had no room in his life for a "relationship"? And she had accepted that — or tried to. If he didn't want a relationship with her, why did he think an explanation was necessary?

She shrugged. "I just don't think an explanation is called for," she said in her mother's most proper voice. "You've made it crystal clear all along that I'm not entitled to any explanations from you."

The evening had turned cool and she was wearing a lightweight cotton blouse. But if she shivered, he'd use that as an excuse for both of them to go inside. She wrapped her arms around her chest for warmth.

"Well, I'm telling you *now* that you *are* entitled to an explanation. You're being silly, refusing to hear it."

He certainly would make a fine lawyer one day, just as Bill said he would. Putting the other person on the defensive was considered, she knew, a good courtroom tactic. She didn't want an explanation. She wanted him to apologize all over the place and beg her forgiveness and promise faithfully that it would never, ever happen again. She wanted him to say that the girl in the red dress was a dreadful bore, a witch, a monster not fit for human companionship. She wasn't interested in hearing anything else. She especially wasn't interested in hearing a calm, rational explanation as to why the boy she loved had been in a local restaurant with a sexy blonde in a red dress, or in hearing a lecture about why she was silly to be angry.

"So, I'm being silly," she said, looking him full in the face. "Isn't that what you think girls my age do best?"

Annoyance spread across his handsome face and before it could develop into full-blown anger, she said, "Look, I've got to go inside. I'm turning the house into a refrigerator. 'Bye." And she closed the door, snapping the lock with a sharp click. Paige and Tuck had their own keys.

This time, she didn't watch him leave. Why torture herself? And although Katie felt that she'd done the right thing, her steps as she climbed the stairs to read a promised story to Megan and Mary Emily were slower, as if she were much older than fifteen.

Tuck's evening didn't progress much better than his sister's. Deciding that it would be a while before Jennifer returned from the out-of-town game, he went to a movie by himself to pass the time. The movie wasn't funny. He found it depressing and left the theater regretting his choice. But what other choice had there been? Everyone he knew was at the game and a movie was the only thing he was willing to attend alone. Consulting his watch as he left the theater, he realized the people at the game wouldn't be back yet.

He drove to Paddy's, knowing everyone would gather there when they returned to town. He parked and waited. He hoped fiercely as he slouched down in the seat that Ed Thomas had had a really bad night quarterbacking.

For the life of him, he couldn't figure out what a bright, popular, beautiful girl like Jennifer Bailey saw in a boob like Ed Thomas.

After a time of depressing solitude filled with grim, angry thoughts, Tuck caught a flash of yellow in his rearview mirror and sat up straight. The school bus stopped in front of Paddy's and spilled out a load of cheering, laughing Harrison High students. Jennifer was a cheerleader and rode the team bus, but he knew now that it would be along shortly. Better to go inside Paddy's now, so it wouldn't look like he'd been waiting in the car.

He found a group of classmates to sit with. Ordinarily, he knew, they would have paid little or no attention to him. Well, the girls might have smiled and said hello. But the guys usually looked right through him. But tonight everyone was in a good mood because of a hard-won victory, so they called out as he entered the restaurant, "Hey, Guthrie, c'mon over!" When they realized Katie wasn't with him and wasn't going to be, some of the boys' faces registered disappointment, but Tuck was already seated by then and they couldn't very well tell him to leave.

Whatever the reason for the invitation, he was grateful. He didn't want to be sitting alone when Jennifer walked in, with or without The Hulk.

Everyone assumed he'd been to the game. He saw no reason to volunteer the information that he'd gone to a movie. He knew, too, he had to be careful not to let on that his parents were out of town. That was a definite no-no.

When Jennifer walked in, her red hair tied up in a curly ponytail, her fair skin flushed with excitement, his heart slammed against his chest. And then quickly sank, as the bulky frame of Ed Thomas appeared close behind her. Tuck frowned. Didn't she ever go anywhere without Dumbo?

The girl sitting beside him, a tiny blonde named Casey, said softly, "Forget it, Guthrie. Thomas has her roped and tied."

Tuck said nothing, his eyes on Jennifer as she moved, smiling, among the tables and booths. In her heavy blue sweater and short cream-colored pleated skirt, she looked, he thought, as pretty as any girl he'd ever seen.

"You know, Guthrie," Casey said in that same quiet voice, "there *are* other girls in Philadelphia."

He looked at her then. She was, in an elfin sort of way, really cute, with short blonde hair, curling closely around her face, and a splattering of freckles across the bridge of her nose. Her eyes, he noticed, were not a warm, velvety brown like Jennifer's. They were instead a brilliant blue. And her mouth, although serious now, looked like it might break into a grin at any moment.

He supposed she wanted him to flirt with her. He didn't want to. He just wasn't good at that stuff.

"Yeah?" he asked brusquely. "Not as far as I'm concerned." He was instantly sorry, as a look of hurt flashed across the pixieish face. "I mean," he began quickly because he really hated hurting her feelings, but she interrupted him, her cheeks scarlet.

"No, that's okay," she said in an artificially cheerful voice, "really. I understand." Then she turned away from him and began a brisk conversation with the person on the other side of her.

Tuck felt as if he were standing alone at the end of a plank suspended above shark-infested waters. Nearly everybody at Harrison disliked him because he was too mannerly. Now he'd offended this nice girl by forgetting his manners. Whichever way he moved, it seemed to be the wrong way. Not only was he making no progress with Jennifer, he had just alienated a perfectly nice girl. Maybe he'd be better off not speaking for the rest of his life.

And then Jennifer Bailey was standing in front of him, asking him what he thought of the game.

"Well, we won, didn't we?" he responded safely.

"Yeah, thanks to good old Ed here!" one of the boys in the booth shouted, getting up to clap an arm around Ed Thomas's substantial shoulders.

And Tuck had to close his eyes for just a second to shut out the look of pride on Jennifer Bailey's beautiful face.

Why was he letting himself in for this kind of punishment, he wondered. Maybe if he could have kept their library date the night Miss Aggie fell, they'd have made some progress by now. But he'd had no choice. He'd had to tell Paige to call Jennifer and explain. And she'd seemed nice enough about it in school the next day. Said she'd understood, that family problems, which was all Paige had told her, were very important.

But maybe she hadn't really understood. Maybe she'd decided that he just wasn't reliable, couldn't be counted on. Maybe she'd decided that she was better off with Neanderthal man, since he was certainly *always* there.

I know she likes me, Tuck thought, watching her chatting and laughing with his classmates. I know she does.

But it was Ed Thomas's hand Jennifer Bailey was holding, not Tucker Guthrie's.

"Gotta go," he said abruptly, jumping to his feet. No one seemed interested in stopping him. Casey didn't even look up. Jennifer flashed him a quick, brilliant smile and just as quickly returned to her conversation.

Tuck went home.

The discussion about the movie Paige and Ben had seen began, as discussions about movies always did for them, with a good-natured argument.

"I almost fell asleep in there," she said casually as they got into Ben's father's car. "Nothing *happened!*"

"Nothing happened? How can you say nothing happened?" Ben slid into the front seat, fastened his safety belt, and turned on the ignition. The engine grumbled for several seconds before dragging itself into action. "The film was about Victorian society. It was about people and morals. Weren't you paying attention?"

"Of course I was paying attention," Paige said indignantly as the car pulled away from the curb. "For a while, anyway. I thought the pond scene was hilarious. And the photography was just beautiful. But there certainly wasn't much of a story, if you ask me."

Then she settled back in her seat while Ben delivered the anticipated lecture about subtlety in films and how a message didn't have to be delivered with a sledgehammer to be effective. She'd heard it all before, and it no longer bothered her. So he liked foreign films, and she didn't particularly. So what? As long as they didn't have major battles over films, they could keep going. She just liked being with him, and occasionally they actually agreed on the merits or drawbacks of a particular film.

"I'm starving!" she said when he had run out of arguments, "Can we eat, please?"

"You weren't listening to a single word I said," he protested mildly.

"I *was* listening!" She grinned. "You were saying that you think I'm absolutely wonderful and brilliant and there is no one you'd rather see a movie with."

He laughed. "Gee, is that what I was saying? Funny, it didn't sound anything like that to me."

"Then you should get your hearing checked. But before you do that, I desperately need a hamburger with everything on it, a large order of fries, and a thick chocolate milkshake, okay?"

Shaking his head but still laughing, Ben drove not to Paddy's, which he disliked, but to a small restaurant close to the theater. "It's quieter here," he said as he got out of the car, "we can talk."

"As long as we don't talk about movies," Paige joked.

They didn't talk about movies. She was always just a little bit nervous about holding up her end of the conversation with Ben. He was so bright and well-informed about current events. Paige considered herself just as informed, and the Whitman/Guthrie family always enjoyed discussions at the evening meal. Still, she worried about being able to express what she thought.

But they had no trouble this night keeping up a steady flow of conversation. One topic she avoided diligently was her family. If she said one word about what had been going on at home, Ben would get that look on his face, as if he'd just bitten into a lemon.

"You have really beautiful eyes, you know that?" he said suddenly, startling her. Ben never said things like that. And she never thought of any of her features as being "beautiful" or even coming close. Most people remarked about Katie's bright blue eyes, and her blonde hair and perfect figure, seldom commenting on Paige's looks.

"No, I didn't know that," she managed. "But thanks. I'm glad you think so."

"Are you?"

She had to look at him then, and was surprised by the expression on his thin face. That expression was serious and intense, which was very like Ben, but it said all the things that he might have difficulty saying aloud. It said, I'm glad I'm here with *you*, Paige, instead of someone else. That look meant a lot to her.

"Yes," she said simply, "I'm very glad you think so."

Then someone in the kitchen dropped a dish, breaking it and their mood. Ben joked about "butter-fingers" and Paige relaxed. But the warm feeling of this moment stayed with her.

"I know a great way home," Ben announced as they left the restaurant, holding hands. "It's a beautiful night, and it will be a nicer ride than the usual one. We'll see a little of the countryside and get home in plenty of time for your curfew."

The engine protested so briskly when he started it this time that Paige said nervously, "Maybe we should just go straight home, Ben. This car sounds a little sick to me."

"Come on, Paige, since when are you a car expert? It's been doing this lately. It's just temperamental, that's all. Needs a new battery, I think. And," he added with a grin as he pulled out into traffic, "if anyone should understand temperamental behavior, you should."

That began a heated discussion that included protestations on Paige's part, teasing on Ben's part, and a certain amount of laughter.

She did enjoy the drive. Every now and then they passed small clusters of houses and one or two larger developments, all dark now. "They must roll up the sidewalks around here at nine o'clock," he commented as he pulled off the main road up the hill onto a dirt road. "Think there are really people living in those houses?"

"Sure. But if they work in town, they must have to get up pretty early to get to work. So they go to bed early. Sounds sensible to me."

There were no houses on the dirt road, although far below them they could see the faint glow of city lights. "Are you sure this road leads somewhere?" Paige finally asked, when they had been driving for what seemed to her an awfully long time. There was no clock in Ben's car and she couldn't see to read her own watch. But it felt late to her. She tried to calculate the time: they'd left the movie theater around nine-thirty or nine forty-five, and how long had they been in the restaurant? An hour? Ninety minutes? And they'd been driving forever!

"I've been on this road a hundred times," he said with a trace of annoyance. "My dad used to bring me up here berry-picking. It comes out close to your house, I promise. But first," pulling the car off to the side of the road, "I want you to see what your city looks like at night from up here in the clouds."

It *was* impressive. They got out and walked to the edge of the cliff, Ben's arm around her shoulder. "I can't tell you what anything is," she commented, shivering slightly in the cool night air, "but it makes a pretty picture, all those glowing lights. It looks huge, doesn't it? The city, I mean."

They stood there for a while, talking about the city in which they'd both grown up.

But Paige was getting increasingly more nervous. She had no idea how much further they had to drive before arriving at her house. Wouldn't Katie just love it if Paige broke curfew? One thing more to tell Virginia Mae and Dad when they got back. "Ben, I think we should go," she said quietly.

"Okay, you're right," he agreed. But instead of turning toward the car, he turned toward her. Lifting her chin with his hand, he bent and kissed her, saying her name first just once. She no longer felt chilly, and curfew was the furthest thing from her mind. Relaxing against him, she returned the kiss, her arms reaching up to encircle his neck.

"Thanks for a nice night," he said as he lifted his head, looking down into her face, smiling.

"Thank *you*," she said lightly, although her knees felt just a little weak.

Taking her hand, he led her back to the car. And bent to kiss her again before she climbed into the front seat. Walking with a light step, he moved around to the front of the car and got in, smiling over at her before turning his attention to the ignition.

He turned the key. Nothing happened. He turned it again. Still nothing. This time there were no grumblings, no rumblings, no sound of any kind.

Curfew or no curfew, it was obvious that they weren't going anywhere in this particular car at this particular time.

Ben kept trying. Unsuccessfully.

I am not, Paige thought with despair, going to make curfew. In fact, from the look of things, I'll be lucky to get home tonight at all.

"Ben!" she cried, "*Do* something!"

CHAPTER 12

Katie awoke in the middle of the night. She wasn't sure if a noise had awakened her or if a bad dream had disturbed her sleep. Had one of the younger girls cried out? Megan occasionally had nightmares.

Struggling out of bed in the darkened room, she pulled on her white terrycloth robe and tiptoed, still half-asleep, to the doorway. Not wanting to awaken Paige, she opened the door gently, but the hinge shrieked a protest. She held her breath. A Paige rudely awakened in the middle of the night would almost certainly resemble a tiger with a thorn in its paw. But a quick, nervous glance across the room toward Paige's bed showed no sign of movement. Good!

Katie moved into the hallway, closed the door behind her, and flicked on the light switch. She listened for sounds and heard nothing but the rumble of her own empty stomach. She had no idea what time it was, but now there'd be no return to sleep without a glass of milk. First things first, she told herself, and padded softly to the younger girls' bedroom.

Nothing. They were both sound asleep, Mary Emily gently snoring, Megan on her stomach, legs and arms splayed in total surrender to sleep. Sighing with relief, Katie walked toward the kitchen.

Paige or Tuck had forgotten to turn off the porch light when they came in. That was the responsibility of whoever trailed in last. Probably Paige, Katie thought matter-of-factly as she gave the switch an effective slap. If curfew is twelve o'clock, she comes in at eleven fifty-nine and not one minute sooner.

The clock in the kitchen read four-twenty. No wonder I'm hungry, Katie thought, zeroing in on the refrigerator, it's almost morning.

With the comforting milk easing her hunger pangs, Katie went back upstairs. As she opened the bedroom door, the hall light bathed the room in a dim glow. She reached quickly for the switch to turn it off.

But not before she realized with a gasp that Paige's bed was . . . empty!

Empty? At four-thirty in the morning? Impossible!

Her hand remained immobile on the light switch. Where was Paige? Not in the kitchen — Katie had just come from there. Not in the living room — she'd passed through it on the way to the kitchen. The bathroom? Of course, the bathroom! That was probably what had awakened

Katie in the first place, Paige getting out of bed.

There were, however, two things wrong with that theory and Katie recognized both of them instantly: the first was that no light shone from beneath the bathroom door. The second and far more important consideration was that Paige's bed was made. It wasn't made well, but it *was* made. Considering the effort it had taken to persuade Paige to make it early that morning, it wasn't at all likely that she would make it when she left it for a few minutes in the middle of the night.

She's not home, Katie thought, fear rising in her chest. Paige never came home tonight.

Katie had no idea what to do. Just to be absolutely sure, she went back downstairs and checked every room on the first floor and both porches. There was no sign of Paige. The porch light had been left on because the last person due home had never arrived.

Katie stood in the center of the living room, clasping and unclasping her hands. I don't know what to do, she thought with barely controlled panic. Should I wake up Tuck? Was there something he could do that she, Katie, couldn't? *Was* there anything to do?

Trying desperately to calm down and think clearly, she sank into a chair. What, she wondered, would Mom do? No answer came, since she couldn't imagine anyone breaking curfew under Virginia Mae's watchful eyes.

Because the strongest fear she had was that Paige had been in an accident, she went to the telephone and called every local hospital. Had there been a patient admitted by the name of Whitman? The answer was the same at every hospital: no there had not.

Well, that was something. Although she could still be lying in a ditch somewhere, unconscious.

Where *was* she?

At that precise moment, Paige was asleep in the front seat of Ben's sedan, her head resting on a sleeping Ben's shoulder. No one had come along to help them, after all, and after countless attempts at starting a dead engine, Ben gave up.

"Look," he'd said calmly to a semi-hysterical Paige, "we have two choices here. We can scream and shout and get crazy because we're stranded, which will do absolutely no good at all, or we can get comfortable and get some sleep. There will be cars on this road in the morning and someone will have battery cables."

Paige had stared at him. She was painfully aware of the passage of time and was sure that she had already missed her curfew. She could only hope that Katie and Tuck were sound asleep in their beds, totally unaware that one member of their family was missing. "You mean stay here all night?" she asked. "We can't do that! We have to get home!"

The faint glow of a full moon overhead played around Ben's face. "How would you suggest we get home?" he asked quietly. "It's hard to hitch-hike when there aren't any cars on the road, and it's too far to walk."

"I thought you said my house wasn't far from here," she argued angrily.

"I meant by car. Not on foot. We're perfectly safe here. I can't say the same for out there," Ben said shrugging in the direction of the darkness surrounding them.

"But my family will be frantic! Can't we at least try to find a telephone?" Paige asked.

"My folks will be worried, too, if they haven't already gone to bed. But look around, Paige. Do you see anything resembling a house? Houses have telephones, right? No houses, no telephone."

"Well, you don't have to be so sarcastic," Paige grumbled. She was thinking about what Katie would make of her being out all night. Good grief, that was all she needed: one more thing for Katie to use against her.

"You and your shortcuts," Paige complained.

"There's nothing wrong with this shortcut," Ben replied with annoyance. "Its a perfectly good shortcut. But the battery in this car is dead and we don't have anyone to jump-start it for us. Don't blame the shortcut."

Paige wasn't ready to give in and accept this intolerable situation. "But if we weren't out in the middle of No-Man's Land, there'd *be* someone to help us, or a telephone we could use."

"Yes, but there *isn't*. Now do you want to sit here and argue all night long or do you want to sleep?"

She wanted to argue. It seemed somehow wrong to give in on something so crucial. And arguing would keep her from thinking about the trouble she was in.

But she was suddenly too tired to keep up the argument. Settling back against the seat, an unfriendly distance between herself and Ben, she decided that Katie and Tuck hadn't even noticed her absence. They had, as she mentally wrote out the safest scenario, gone to bed early. And if there was any justice in the world at all, someone would come along at the crack of dawn to jump-start Ben's battery. She'd get back into the house before anyone was awake and busy herself in the kitchen. If Katie wanted to know what on earth she was doing up so early, she'd think of something. Something simple would be best: she'd been hungry, that was it. Too hungry to sleep. That way, as soon as she ate something, she could go upstairs. Katie would think she was going *back* to bed.

That was when she'd remembered that she'd made her bed that morning. If Katie woke up and saw that, Paige could hardly say she'd just come downstairs for something to eat. But she had no intention of staying up all day without any sleep. Okay, so she'd have to say she'd intended to stay up and that's why she'd made her bed. Then a headache would come on and she'd feel the need to go back to bed. That, weak as it was, would have to do.

"I didn't do this on purpose," Ben said. He was slouched down in the seat, his head tilted back.

Startled, she looked over at him. "I know that!" In fact, it hadn't occurred to her that he might have planned such a thing. Some boys, she knew, would have. But not Ben.

"Well, I just wanted to be sure you knew that."

She felt sorry for him then. This couldn't be the way he'd planned the evening to end. And his

parents would be worried, too. And didn't everyone always think that guys were supposed to know
how to fix situations like this? That really wasn't
fair, was it? This wasn't Ben's fault, and there
wasn't anything he could do about it.

Erasing the distance between them by sliding
across the front seat, she reached over and took
his hand. "It's okay," she said, "really." He
squeezed her hand gratefully. "I mean," she said,
leaning against him, "it could be worse. Virginia
Mae and Dad could be waiting for me when I
finally drag into the house tomorrow morning."

It *was* kind of funny — the honeymoon trip
she'd dreaded had turned into a blessing. "All I'll
have to deal with is Katie. And Tuck, of course.
I can handle them." Oh, sure, a little voice inside
her sneered, and pigs have wings. Ignoring that,
she snuggled against Ben and closed her eyes.
And didn't object when he slipped an arm around
her and pulled her closer.

Back at the house, Katie decided to call the
police. Wasn't that what you did when someone
wasn't where she was supposed to be? Paige was
supposed to be home, and she wasn't.

But hadn't Bill said once that the police never
look for a missing person until the person had
been missing twenty-four hours? Katie had
strongly and loudly disapproved of that policy
when he'd mentioned it. "Well, that's just ridiculous!" she had argued. "All kinds of terrible
things could happen to a person in twenty-four
hours! Why don't they look for them right away?"

He had explained that most missing persons were runaways who left of their own free will and returned quickly.

Could Paige have run away? Could she have been so disgusted with the way things were going that she'd left her own home and family? No, that was just plain silly. She hadn't seemed at all angry when she'd left the house. At least, no more so than usual.

There was no point in calling Ben's house. Since Paige wasn't home, Ben couldn't be, either. And his parents would be sound asleep. Why wake them up and get them all worried? That would be cruel and it certainly wouldn't do anyone any good.

Miss Aggie often said, "No news is good news." In this case, wouldn't that mean that if Paige had had an accident, the family would be notified right away and since they hadn't been, Paige was still in one piece? The police hadn't called or come to the house to say that she was lying in a ditch somewhere. And no hospital had called to say that she was lying in a hospital bed, broken and bruised.

Then why wasn't she home where she belonged? Just exactly where *was* Paige Elizabeth Whitman at five o'clock on a Saturday morning?

Katie Summer shook her head vigorously. The thought that had just popped into her head wasn't acceptable. Paige wasn't foolish. She liked Ben. Maybe she even loved him. But she wouldn't do anything as crazy as spending the night with a boy. Her parents would kill her. Paige had her

117

future pretty well planned. She was going to study Journalism at college and she hoped to work for a big newspaper one day. Katie knew that. She wouldn't take a chance on throwing all of that away just for a boy. Not Paige.

Then Katie remembered that Paige had been without a mother for a long, long time. Was it possible that someone as smart as Paige didn't *know* how being careless could mess up your life? Katie knew that some of the girls at school believed some pretty silly things about what happened with boys, none of them having any basis in biology. She had no idea where they got such unreal ideas. Her own mother had told her the right facts a long time ago, and she was grateful for that, and she'd had classes in school, too.

She shook her head again. Paige was just too smart not to know. She'd taken all kinds of biology courses.

Still . . . if Paige were feeling truly left out because of the marriage and now the honeymoon, well, sometimes people did dumb things. Maybe Paige was one of them.

Although her eyes finally closed, Katie slept fitfully in the chair until a key twisting in the front door woke her.

Ben had been right about early-morning traffic. A farmer headed into town for his monthly supplies was kind enough to jump-start the ailing battery.

"What are you going to tell your parents?" Paige asked as they drove toward home. She was cold and stiff and so hungry her stomach felt hollow. Or maybe, she thought, that was just from fear.

"The truth, what else? My dad knows this battery has been throwing tantrums."

Paige's temper flared. "You said something like that earlier," she complained, "and what I want to know is, *why* didn't you get a new battery?"

"Because they're not *free*. And I thought it would hold out a while longer. So what are you going to tell Katie about tonight?"

Paige shrugged. "I'm not going to tell her anything."

Ben shot her a surprised look. "She's probably been worried sick. It wouldn't kill you to fill her in on what happened."

Paige moved away from his side. This whole night seemed like some stupid nightmare, and she still had Katie and Tuck to face. And there sat Ben, talking to her as if she were a naughty five-year-old being mean to her four-year-old sister.

"It's none of her business where I was or what I was doing. She doesn't tell me every last detail of *her* life." The car was beginning to climb up the hill to her house. The sun was up, and Paige fervently hoped Katie wasn't. Tuck definitely wouldn't be. He believed that early Saturday mornings were good for only one thing: sleeping.

"If you don't tell her the truth," Ben said as he made a left turn into the steep driveway, "you can't blame her for any conclusions she draws."

"That's ridiculous," Paige said.

"Oh, come on, Paige, we *were* out all night. And everyone knows you're crazy about me."

119

He grinned. "You can't very well explain that it was all perfectly innocent if you don't intend to say anything."

"Oh, honestly, Ben, Katie is not going to think anything like that!"

He parked the car, still grinning. "Oh, yeah? She might not realize what a perfect gentleman I am."

Paige managed to laugh. "There isn't a single thing about you that's perfect! And this whole conversation is just plain crazy. I'm going inside. Thanks for a really interesting evening. Maybe I'll write about it someday."

"Yeah, well if you do, change my name. I wouldn't want the whole world to think I'm a wimp. Not taking advantage of the situation, I mean."

"Ben! Come on! See you later. I hope your folks don't give you a hard time."

He shrugged as she slid across the seat and opened the door. "No problem. *I'm* going to explain."

As she was walking up the steps, he called out the window, "Get some sleep. I don't want you cranky when I call later."

She sent him a smile and waved as he backed out of the driveway. Then, taking a deep breath, she put her key in the front door lock, turned it, and pushed the door open as quietly as possible.

She found a white-faced, visibly shaken Katie standing in the foyer facing her.

CHAPTER 13

Where on earth have you been?" Katie Summer demanded, her voice low but quivering.

Paige pushed the door closed. She moved on into the living room, tossing her jacket on the couch. "Out," she said, and headed for the kitchen.

Katie followed her, anger canceling out her usual grace, stiffening her movements. "Paige, I want an explanation. I've been worried sick about you." Paige was pouring a glass of milk, her back to Katie. Katie's voice rose slightly. "I woke up at four-thirty and you weren't here. So I couldn't go back to sleep. I called the hospitals to see if you'd been in an accident."

"Well, that was clever of you." Paige turned to leave the kitchen, glass of milk and some graham crackers in hand, but Katie blocked her exit.

"Oh, no you don't! You're not leaving this room until I get an explanation."

Paige was wearing heeled boots while Katie was in her bare feet. Looking down at her stepsister's pale, drawn face, bluish circles from a restless night under her eyes, Paige felt a wash of guilt sweep over her. "We had car trouble."

"*Car* trouble? All night long? Why didn't Ben call his father? Or Tuck? Or a wrecker?"

Paige shrugged. So much for explaining. If Katie was going to demand a play-by-play account of the evening, she could just forget it. Well, at least she'd tried. "Move out of my way, please. I need some sleep."

"Paige!"

"Good *night*, Katie. Or should I say good morning? Whatever . . ." Paige brushed by Katie, who hesitated, then followed her. "Paige, is there some reason you won't tell me what happened?"

Paige said nothing until she reached the stairs and had started up them. Then, halfway up, she turned and regarded Katie coldly. "I *told* you what happened."

The coldness in Paige's voice brought furious color to Katie's pale face.

"Katie, you really should comb your hair. It's all . . . wrinkled." And with that, Paige continued on up the stairs and disappeared.

Katie stood at the bottom of the stairs, tears in her eyes. Paige was absolutely hateful. Just hateful. I was entitled to an explanation, she thought as she returned to the kitchen. *I'm* the one who sat up half the night waiting for her. *I'm* the one who was worried sick. She *owes* me.

But Paige obviously had no intention of paying.

Needing action, she made a cup of tea and toasted two slices of wheat bread. Then she sat at the kitchen table and played with the toast until it looked as if it had just come from a blender instead of a toaster.

Putting her feet up on an empty chair, she stirred her tea and wondered if she should tell Tuck that Paige had been out all night. She decided not to. One thing Paige didn't need was any more ammunition against Katie, and telling Tuck would definitely fall into that category. Besides, the way Tuck had been acting lately, he probably wouldn't even listen while Katie was talking. It was as if he wanted nothing to do with anyone in this family. He never talked to her anymore, never told her what was going on in his life or how he felt about it. The only thing she knew for sure about him was that he wasn't happy. But she didn't know why, not really. Okay, Jennifer had something to do with it. But that couldn't be all of it, because he'd been acting funny even before Jennifer came into the picture.

She missed him. Once upon a time, he had been interested in *her* life, especially right after her father had left. She'd needed Tuck then, and he'd been there for her. She still needed him, only not as much. Maybe he thought she didn't need him at all, now that Bill was around. Maybe she should talk to him, set him straight. Sometime.

When Megan and Mary Emily came into the kitchen, a beautiful fall morning putting extra bounce in their steps, they found Katie sitting at the table staring into a steaming cup of tea.

"Katie looks sad," Megan commented quietly as she pulled a box of cereal from the cupboard.

"No, she's just thinking," Mary Emily said. "Let's not bother her. I'll get the milk. You make some toast, okay?"

Katie heard none of that. She was wondering how she was going to get through the day. It stretched ahead of her, long, blurry, headachey hours of caring for the younger sisters, of housecleaning and worst of all, of no Jake. It was only seven-thirty in the morning. Tuck would sleep late, and Paige probably wouldn't crawl out of bed until after noon. Katie was on her own, something she was in no shape to be.

Then there was the promised phone call to Hawaii. How on earth was she going to sound cheerful when she talked to her mother and Bill? When she felt like she'd just gone through the washing machine and dryer, on Extra-Full Load.

"I'm going to get dressed," she said and went to do just that.

"We need to cheer up Katie," Mary Emily suggested when she and Megan were alone. "Think of something we can do that will make her feel better."

"Like what? And what's wrong with her, anyway?"

Mary Emily frowned. "I guess she had a fight with Jake. That's the way she always looks when she's had a fight with Jake. But I know something we can do to cheer her up."

"What?"

"We'll clean up the kitchen. We'll unload the

dishwasher's load from last night and load it again and we'll mop the floor. . . ."

"The floor isn't dirty, Mary Emily. Tuck mopped it last night."

Mary Emily looked temporarily confused. Then, "Well, we'll just clean everything else. Then Katie won't have to do anything at all. That will make her feel better, don't you think?"

Megan agreed, and by the time Katie came back downstairs, the kitchen sparkled.

Katie *was* touched. A clean kitchen didn't change the fact that Paige, for whatever reason, had been out all night. And it wouldn't bring Jake knocking at her door. But it meant that two people, Megan and Mary Emily, cared about how she felt. That was certainly worth something, wasn't it?

She couldn't disappoint them. Making a deliberate effort to cheer up, she thanked them profusely. "And as a reward," she told their beaming faces, "We'll all go to the park. That will make the time go faster until we can call Hawaii. But first, I have to make a few phone calls, okay?"

While they ran upstairs to put on sweaters, Katie called Sara, Diane, and Lisa. "I want you to come over tonight. We'll go get ice cream and then we'll come back here for a while. I can't believe my mother was serious when she said *no* company allowed. I mean, you guys have to be okay. I've had a rotten week and I'm in desperate need of some friendly companionship, okay?" They all agreed, and she hung up the phone with a sigh of relief. She decided that she wouldn't tell them about Paige. She couldn't do that. In fact, she didn't plan to talk about her family at all. Too depressing! They'd find better things to talk about.

Feeling almost cheerful, she took her younger sisters to the park.

Paige awoke at noon, feeling as if she'd been run over by a very large truck. Remembering her reaction to Katie's questions, she bit her lower lip. I should be ashamed of myself, she thought, sitting up in bed. Katie had every right to be worried. I was supposed to be home by twelve, and instead I was out all night long. Ben was right: it wouldn't have killed me to explain it to her.

But I *did*, she thought in the next second. I *told* her we had car trouble.

She got up and went to the full-length mirror on the closet door. You didn't *really* explain, her slim, dark-haired reflection accused. You could have told her the whole story. You could have put some effort into it. Unless . . . dark brown eyes gazed back at her . . . unless you really *wanted* her to think what she's thinking. *Did* you?

Paige's mind replied indignantly, Of course not! I don't want her thinking any such thing!

But her heart wasn't so sure. There was something just a tiny bit satisfying about Katie not knowing the truth. And it *was* comforting to know that for once, Katie Summer Guthrie was absolutely, positively wrong.

Tossing her bedspread haphazardly over her

crumpled sheets, Paige left her room to take a shower.

At the park, Megan and Mary Emily explored happily while Katie plunked her weary body down on a bench. She had just realized that her red cardigan was buttoned wrong, one side of the hem lower than the other. Coach had been right about the necessity of a good night's sleep. Her brain, overloaded with worry and exhausted from lack of sleep couldn't even remember how to match buttons with buttonholes!

"Hi."

Katie's head swivelled. Jake, astride a silver racing bicycle, had stopped just short of her bench. Fumbling at the buttons on her sweater, she managed to say a soft, "Oh, hello. What are you doing here?"

He laughed. In a Harrison High gray sweatshirt and old denims, he straddled the bike, an amused smile on his face. "I think I'm bike-riding."

Katie felt stupid. She forced a laugh. "I can see that. I just meant — "

"It's okay. I saw you sitting here, and I figured this was a good time to tell you I'm coming over to see you tonight."

Katie jumped up. "Oh, no, you're not!"

"Oh, yes, I am! We need to talk."

He looked disgustingly wonderful, his cheekbones a healthy red from his ride, his dark hair blown every which way. But she had too many other things on her mind to deal with this now.

"I'm busy tonight," she said coolly, her eyes scanning the park for her sisters. There they were, talking to an elderly woman with a large, hairy dog. "I have plans."

"No problem. I'll come over late."

"No!" She'd spoken too sharply. She wanted so much to be casual. That seemed important. "Really. Some other night, maybe."

"Nope!" he said cheerfully, "Tonight! See you then. 'Bye!" And he pedalled away, strong legs pumping, back straight.

She watched him go. I am *not*, she thought decisively, staying home and waiting for him to show up tonight. I'm going to do exactly what I planned to do. I'm going for ice cream with my friends. Jake Carson can sit on my front porch until his hair turns gray!

"Megan! Mary Emily! Come on. It's time to go!"

When Katie walked into the bedroom she shared with Paige, she looked around the un-occupied room and sagged against the doorframe, totally disgusted. Her own bed was still unmade, her pajamas and robe tossed across the bed. She'd been in a hurry when she dressed, she remembered, not wanting to keep Megan and Mary Emily waiting too long. It had seemed far more crucial to take a wake-up shower than to straighten up her room.

But Paige had no such excuse, did she? The girls had been in the park with Katie when Paige finally hauled herself out of bed. Yet her side of the room was in its normal state of chaos. Katie made an impatient sound before attacking her own disarray. She simply didn't feel like getting into it with Paige, not today.

But it *was* Saturday. No school, no swim team practice, no newspaper work. It was the perfect time to give the house a cleaning. Getting Paige to help on what she considered her "day off" wouldn't be easy. I would rather chew on nails, Katie thought as she fluffed her pillow, than ask Paige to help. But I'm going to ask her, anyway.

Because of the time difference, they couldn't call Hawaii until mid-afternoon. At lunch, Katie broached the subject of a housecleaning. "If we don't do it today," she pointed out to a frowning Paige and an uninterested Tuck, "we'll have to do it tomorrow."

Paige took a sip of her milk, deciding it might be wise not to antagonize Katie any further with that Hawaii phone call coming up. She said quickly, "If we absolutely *have* to clean this place, I'd rather get it over with today."

"I second that," Tuck agreed. "I've got nothing going on today, but," with light sarcasm, "who knows what wonderful adventures tomorrow might bring, right?"

Paige could tell Katie hadn't said a word to him about *her* adventure of the night before. Her silence was just one more reason Paige raised no objection at the prospect of scrubbing and polishing. She knew she owed her stepsister, although the idea of such a debt was distasteful.

Katie's face filled with relief. "Great! That's settled then. We'll get started right after lunch." She waited a moment before adding, "by the way," casually, very casually, "Diane and Lisa and Sara are coming over tonight. We're going to get some studying done, after we go out for ice cream."

Paige looked up. "You can't have people over! Don't you remember what your mother said?"

"Yes, I remember. But I don't think she _really_ meant my best friends, especially when we're just going to be studying."

"She _said_," Paige said sharply, "_no_ guests in the house. What makes you think she didn't mean _your_ friends?"

"She's _my_ mother!" Katie snapped in fury, partly because she had a sneaking suspicion that Paige had a point. "And _I_ ought to know what she _really_ meant."

Paige hated that argument, that Virginia Mae was Katie's mother and not Paige's. Katie didn't use it very often, but when she did, it worked. It shut Paige up.

Well, what did she care if Katie was going to be stupid enough to disobey Virginia Mae's direct order? It might make the phone call this afternoon less of a risk. If Katie mentioned last night, Paige could just mention tonight, and what Katie was planning. Fair was fair, after all.

A worried expression on her face, Megan asked anxiously, "Katie, you didn't forget about calling Daddy, did you?"

"No, honey," Katie answered warmly, grateful for the change in subject, "but we can't call Hawaii until later this afternoon. So we might as well stay busy until then, right? That'll make the time go faster."

Megan brightened at that and when she'd finished her lunch, she ran for the can of furniture polish and a dust cloth.

Paige was unable to share Megan's enthusiasm. This business of cleaning the whole house when it was just going to get dirty again seemed totally pointless. Dusting here and there and vacuuming made sense, of course. You couldn't just let dust and dirt build up until it buried you. But Katie actually intended to move the furniture so she could vacuum underneath it! What kind of visitors looked *under* furniture? "Whoever they are," she muttered as she waved a cloth across a book shelf, "I don't want them in *my* house!"

"Paige," Katie said sternly, "you're not supposed to be *patting* the shelves. You're supposed to be dusting them. That means the dustcloth has to come into contact with the shelf."

Paige delivered a withering glance in Katie's direction, but she did apply more pressure to the cloth. How does she *do* that? she wondered angrily. How does she manage to make me feel like I'm *younger* than her? I *hate* that! I'm glad I didn't explain about last night. She doesn't deserve it.

Paige felt the phone call looming over her like a sword about to drop. One wrong word from Katie and she'd be grounded until her old age.

But as it turned out, it wasn't Katie whose remarks caused turmoil during the telephone call to Hawaii. It was Megan.

By two forty-five that afternoon, the house was immaculate. Paige was tired and cranky, Tuck was bored and cranky, and Katie was tired but pleased and not at all cranky. And the house was, as Paige put it, "so clean you could perform surgery in any room."

"Okay, guys," Katie told the two younger girls, "it's morning in Hawaii now. Mom and Bill probably won't have left their room yet to go sightseeing. This is the best time to call, so let's get to it."

Their parents were delighted that they had called. Although Paige held her breath while Katie spoke briefly to her mother, that conversation revealed nothing about the night before, and Paige exhaled deeply when Katie handed the phone to Tuck. Tuck chose to say only, "Hi. I'm fine and I don't have anything exciting to say, so I'll let the small fry have my time."

Mary Emily would have talked indefinitely if Megan hadn't begun tugging at her shoulder. Reluctantly, Mary Emily said good-bye and gave the phone to Megan.

"Mommy?" The delight in Megan's face made her sisters and brother smile. Maybe now, Paige thought, she'll become her old self again, now that she knows Virginia Mae and Dad are just fine. With that worry and the concern about what Katie might have told her parents removed from Paige's mind, she wasn't really paying attention to Megan's conversation. Until she heard the words, "And I've been helping with the housework ever since Miss Aggie fe — "

Tuck clapped a hand over Megan's mouth, and silence descended upon the room.

CHAPTER 14

Megan's eyes widened as she realized what she had almost done. They could all hear Virginia Mae calling, "Megan? Megan! What about Miss Aggie?" And they could hear quite clearly the alarm in her voice.

Thinking quickly out of sheer desperation, Paige hissed into Megan's ear, "Tell her 'ever since Miss Aggie showed me how to use the washing machine and dryer.' Hurry!"

Tuck removed his hand and Megan did as Paige had instructed, making a visible effort to keep her voice steady. And the people around her sagged in relief as Virginia Mae's, "Oh, that's great, honey" reached their ears through the telephone around which they were all huddled.

There was truth in what Paige had told Megan to say. Miss Aggie had, before her fall, instructed both younger girls on the proper use of the new laundry appliances Virginia Mae had bought.

And Megan had, in fact, done several loads of laundry. So they hadn't had to lie. Not really.

But in the next instant, Megan was saying, "No, honest, everything's great!" and, a moment later, "Honest, we're doing just fine." Paige exchanged a nervous glance with Tuck. Why was Megan protesting so much? Had Virginia Mae heard something in her voice? Something they hadn't wanted her to hear?

"My turn," Paige said firmly, taking the receiver. "Virginia Mae? Hi! I guess you're having a great time. We are, too, so don't worry. But we've got to hang up now. This is costing a fortune. Love to Dad. 'Bye!"

Tuck glowered at her as she set down the receiver. "You probably made her more suspicious with that speedy good-bye than Megan did with her goof."

"I'm sorry," Megan apologized. "I didn't mean it. It just slipped out."

"It's okay," Paige told her, patting her shoulder. "We covered just fine." To Tuck she said, "Don't be silly. We'd talked long enough. Dad will be relieved that he won't have to take out a second mortgage on the house to pay the phone bill. Quit worrying, will you? You're worse than your mother."

That was exactly the wrong thing to say. Tuck already resented Virginia Mae and her insistence on the good manners that had affected his reception at Harrison High so negatively. The last thing in the world he wanted right now was to be compared to his mother.

"Thanks, Paige!" he spit out before turning on

his heel and leaving the room, heading for the front porch.

"Paige!" Katie began to scold, but Paige was already on her way upstairs.

Megan and Mary Emily followed Paige. Katie was just about to call Lisa when the telephone rang. It was Lisa.

"Katie? Listen . . . ah . . . didn't you say we were going out for ice cream tonight? And then the four of us were going to hang out at your house?"

"Sure. Why?"

Lisa hesitated for a moment. "Well, I was just at the mall and Danny Sheffield and Pete Graves were there and they said something about coming to your house tonight. You didn't invite them, did you?"

"No, of course not. I don't even *know* Danny Sheffield."

"Sure, you do. He's tall and skinny and has red hair. He's on the basketball team."

"Lisa, I know what he looks like. But I don't *know* him. Why would I invite someone I don't know to my house? Besides, if I'm not supposed to even have you guys in, I certainly wouldn't be inviting more people. They must have been talking about someone else."

"Yeah, right, there are just so many Katie Summers in this town. Could have been any one of them."

Katie almost started worrying after she'd hung up the phone. Why had Danny Sheffield been talking about her? But then she told herself Lisa had simply heard wrong. In spite of what her friends and the kids at school had said, it was beyond Katie's comprehension that anyone would visit someone without an invitation.

The exception to that being, of course, Jake Carson. Jake had dropped in more than once without an invitation, and in fact, might be planning the same move that very evening. Once she hadn't minded.

But that was then, she thought angrily, and this is now. And Jake wasn't any more welcome now without an invitation than Danny Sheffield or Pete Graves.

Wiping Lisa's phone call from her mind, Katie went upstairs to see what Megan and Mary Emily were up to.

The next phone call that came to the Whitman house was for Paige. It was Ben.

"So, how did it go this morning?" he wanted to know.

Paige sat on a high stool in the kitchen, grateful that she had the room all to herself. "Okay. Katie was up, though. She got up during the night and discovered she wasn't sharing the room with anyone, and panicked, I guess. She was waiting for me when I walked in the door."

"Yeah? What'd you tell her?"

"Exactly what I said I was going to tell her. Nothing."

"Paige. . . . "

"Well, I did tell her we had car trouble."

"Oh, good. I thought you said you told her nothing. So, is it okay between you and her?"

Paige knew it wasn't. And she knew Ben was imagining words of explanation that she had never uttered to Katie. "How should I know?" Then, after a moment, "No, I don't think it is. She's been looking at me funny all day. Like I'd lied about the car trouble or something."

"Then you didn't explain very well. And you obviously *let* her think it."

Paige was petulant. "I can't help what she thinks. I have no control over the girl's imagination."

"You did in this instance. All you had to do was tell her exactly what happened. Or," his voice deepened, "exactly what *didn't* happen."

She couldn't pretend she didn't know what he meant.

"I want you to explain it to her, Paige. I'm involved in this, too, and I'm not really keen on Katie thinking something happened when it didn't. So clear it up for her, okay? Tell your sister the truth."

Paige wished fiercely that Ben didn't care what Katie Summer Guthrie thought. "*Step*sister," she snapped. "You keep forgetting."

"I didn't forget." And, after a moment, "I'm coming over there tonight. And I'll be able to tell from Katie's expression whether or not you talked to her. So take care of it, okay?"

"Oh, all right!" At least she would see him tonight. Two nights in a row! "I just don't see why you're making such a big deal out of a little misunderstanding." Then, before he could say anything else, she added, "We have to sit out on the porch, though. I can't invite you in." She said nothing about Katie disobeying Virginia Mae's orders.

"That's okay. It's warm enough. We won't freeze. See you then."

Paige sat with the phone in her hand after he'd hung up. She had no intention of explaining anything about last night to Katie. Maybe Ben could tell from Katie's expression, but Katie would be in the house, and Ben wouldn't. He'd be on the porch. In fact, he'd be on the back porch — less chance that way of running into Katie at all. Good. Because there was simply no way Paige was going to walk up to Katie and say, "Nothing happened last night." She just wasn't ready to do that. Not yet.

Dinner was more cheerful than usual. Megan had relaxed in spite of her slip of the tongue on the phone. She had said to Paige at least three times that afternoon, "Mom and Daddy sounded fine, didn't they, Paige?" Recognizing Megan's relief and delighting in her new-found hearty appetite, Paige forgave her younger sister the little mistake on the phone. Taking the chance that someone might mention Miss Aggie's fall had been worth it, because Megan was her old happy, hungry self again.

And Paige had apologized to Tuck for accusing him of worrying as much as his mother, receiving for her efforts a grudging forgiveness in the form of a brusque, "Forget it, okay?" Better than nothing, she figured, and let it go at that.

As for Katie, she had decided to speak to Paige as little as possible in the four days remaining of their parents' absence. She had no idea what had really happened to Paige and Ben the night before, but she wasn't going to beg for an explanation. The fact that she was entitled to one seemed an opinion not shared by her stepsister.

Fine, she thought, finishing her dinner, fine. If that's the way she wants it, fine! Me, I'm going out tonight, and I'm putting all thoughts of Paige Elizabeth Whitman and all thoughts of Jake Carson out of my mind!

At least for tonight, she thought sheepishly as she took her dishes to the sink, because she knew keeping both those individuals off her mind for long would be impossible.

Remembering Jake's promise in the park to drop in on her that night and anxious to avoid him, she hurried to clean up the kitchen, with Megan's help. Then she ran upstairs to shower and dress in navy corduroy pleated trousers and a pale blue sweater with a white-lace collar. Even though she was just going out with her friends, knowing that she looked nice always perked up her spirits.

And it worked even on this evening when she was disgusted with Paige and jittery about the possibility of running into Jake. By the time she left the house with her friends, they were commenting on her good mood.

"You sounded so desperate on the phone this afternoon," Lisa commented, "I thought you'd be as cranky as a caged tiger."

"Me, too," Sara added. "You sounded like you were ready to tear out your hair."

Katie laughed. "I did. This is a wig."

Laughing, they hurried down the street toward a small cluster of stores at the bottom of the hill.

* * *

After a certain amount of hilarity caused by a rambunctious pillow fight, Megan and Mary Emily allowed Paige to tuck them into bed and turn out the light. Then she went downstairs to wait for Ben.

Tuck returned to his room, turned on his stereo, and flopped across his bed. From there, he could see the stars through his window. He knew Jennifer was probably out there somewhere, since it was Saturday night. But as much as he wanted to see her, the thought of a replay of last night's events made his skull throb. True, he could run into her if he haunted the usual spots. But also true, she'd probably be attached to the arm of Ed Thomas. Also true, she might very well give this southern gentleman a cheerful smile and nothing more.

So what was the point? Better to sack out in his room and count stars. They had been up there in the sky forever and watching them made him feel small and unimportant. Insignificant. But he felt that way most of the time these days, anyway.

His room, at least, was one place he belonged. There weren't many of those since they'd left Atlanta.

Katie and her friends decided to splurge on both calories and finances by ordering the Black Mountain Decadence, a monstrous sundae ladled thick with chocolate syrup, marshmallow creme, pineapple tidbits, and two kinds of nuts.

"You're breaking training," Sara pointed out to Katie, a wicked grin on her face.

"I know it. But after this past week, I deserve a treat. Besides" — returning the grin — "they don't have veggies on the menu here."

"True, true. Okay, we won't tell on you. So dig in!"

"Uh-oh," Lisa said suddenly, "aspiring lawyer on the left!"

Puzzled, Katie lifted her head. And turned to see Jake Carson entering the restaurant. Was he following her?

"I think he's following you," Diane said. "This is getting pretty routine, him showing up wherever you are. Maybe he bugged your phone to find out where you'd be at all times. Don't lawyers know about stuff like that?"

"He's not a lawyer," Katie muttered, her head once again bent over her sundae. "And lawyers don't do that kind of stuff, detectives do it."

To her relief, Jake stayed at the front counter. This information was relayed to her by Diane, who sat facing front. "He's ordering a cone, I think," she whispered. Then, "Chocolate, I think. Wait . . . he's getting sprinkles, too."

"Diane," Katie hissed, "I am not the slightest bit interested in what Jake Carson's ice cream choices are!"

Undaunted, Diane continued, "He's getting his cone. He's paying for it."

"Diane! Cut it out!" But Katie couldn't repress a giggle. Diane sounded like a sportscaster giving a play-by-play account of an athletic event.

"He's looking this way. Wow, Katie, he really *is* gorgeous. I don't blame you for being dippy about him."

"DI-*ANE*! I am *not* dippy about him!" She giggled again. "Southern girls do not get dippy about guys. Everyone knows it's the other way around."

"He's coming this way. No, he's not. Yes, he is. No, he's turning. He's leaving. Katie, he's *leaving*!"

"I don't care," Katie said calmly.

The fact that her Black Mountain Decadence suddenly lost its appeal was almost certainly due to guilt over breaking training. It almost certainly had nothing to do with Jake Carson's silent departure.

Fifteen minutes later, with a great deal of groaning and a good many promises to never eat another bite of food again, they left the ice cream store and began the uphill climb to Katie's house. A line of cars snaking up the hill lit their way.

"Somebody must be having a party," Katie commented as they reached the halfway mark. "We don't usually have this much traffic on our street."

When they were just a few houses away from their destination, she added, "It must be the people next door. Most of these cars are parking near our house."

When they reached her house, where cars were maneuvering for parking places on the street and pulling into the long, narrow Whitman driveway, Lisa turned to Katie and said slowly, "Now I think I know what Pete Graves and Danny Sheffield meant today at the mall. Because unless I'm very much mistaken, Katie, *you're* the one giving a party tonight!"

CHAPTER 15

Katie couldn't seem to find her voice. She watched silently, eyes wide, as Harrison High School students began pouring out of cars and milling around in the street, laughing and shouting hellos to one another.

"Katie, you'd better do something!" Sara advised. "And you'd better do it fast. Because I think Lisa's right. I think you're having a party."

Katie snapped to attention. "No, I'm not. I am *not*!" Grabbing Lisa's elbow, she urged her friends up the steps and onto the porch. They stood there, watching in dismay as a sea of people congregated at the foot of the steep staircase.

"Hey, Guthrie!" a boy's voice called. "Here we are! Let the games begin!"

"Go away!" Katie called. "There isn't any party! There never *was* a party! You've all made a mistake."

The boy laughed. "No mistake here," he called. "Listen, don't sweat it! We brought our own stuff." He held up a styrofoam cooler, as did half a dozen other people standing behind him. "All we need is your home sweet home."

"Well, you can't have it!" Under the glare of the porch light, Katie's face was drawn and tense. "My parents aren't home and no one's allowed in." She knew she wasn't telling them anything they didn't already know. They wouldn't have come in the first place if they hadn't heard about the Hawaiian trip. Her friends had been right, and she wished now she had taken them more seriously. It wouldn't have changed the current situation, but at least she'd have been prepared. She could have turned off all the inside lights and pretended no one was home.

Paige and Ben, who had been out in the garden, joined Katie and her friends on the porch just as the first wave of party-seekers landed on the top step. Katie recognized several members of the football team. Looking at their flushed faces, she thought, I'm not the only athlete who broke training tonight. At least *I* did it with ice cream, not beer.

"Katie!" Paige cried. "What's going on? What are all these people doing here?" A second later, Tuck appeared behind her, holding the front door open as he took in the scene.

"I don't — " Katie began, but one of the uninvited guests interrupted her.

"Hey, Paige, how's it going? Listen," he said in a very friendly voice, "don't worry about a thing. We brought our own eats and," with a wink to his companions, "even our own liquid refreshment." Then he stepped onto the porch with a backward wave of his hand to signal onward the throng of people behind him.

"Well," Tuck said in a firm voice, "you'll have to eat your eats and drink your drinks someplace else, because this house is not receiving guests tonight."

The boy Katie regarded as the "leader of the pack" laughed. "Hey, did you hear that, folks?" he called. "They're not receiving guests. Oh, boy, Guthrie, the way you talk! That just knocks me out."

"Don't tempt me," Tuck said from between clenched teeth.

"Gee, I'm really scared. Look at me, I'm shakin'!" More laughter from the crowd.

Tuck took a step forward, his jaw clenched. But Ben reached out to stop him. "Look, guys," Ben told the dozen or so people on the porch and top step, "you can see there's been a mistake. There's no party here tonight." He waved toward the crowd filling most of the steps leading up to the house. "Take your party to someone else's house."

Katie thought Ben sounded totally in charge, and heaved a sigh of relief.

Too soon, because in the next instant the crowd's leader said hotly, "We came here to have a party and we're going to have a party. So stop being a drag, Collins, and move out of the way." Then he turned and waved to the crowd, calling, "C'mon, everyone, party time!"

There were too many of them to stop. Ben and

Tuck, even with the five girls, were no match for sixty people bent on having a party in this particular house at this particular time. Before Katie could call out, Tuck had been pushed out of the way, and a stream of laughing, cooler-carrying people were making their way into the yellow Victorian house that Katie's mother had said no one could enter in her absence.

The people who did belong in the house and their friends watched in dumbfounded silence as couple upon couple entered through the doorway. Tuck wasn't really shocked to spot a laughing Jennifer Bailey in the pack. She was with Ed Thomas, which was certainly no shock, either. "You're not supposed to be here," he said in a low voice as she passed him. She threw him an apologetic look and a sweet smile and went on into the house. So much for that, he thought, a sour taste in his mouth. He had thought she was different from the rest of the mob. Maybe he'd been wrong.

"So, what are we going to do?" Tuck asked the others.

"Call the police," Ben suggested. The last of the crowd had gone inside. Katie groaned as she heard someone trip over something and go crashing to the hardwood floor. Screams of laughter followed the fall.

"We can't do that," Sara protested. "We'll all get into trouble. My parents will never believe we didn't invite this crowd here, and I promised them we wouldn't be having a party just because Katie's parents were out of town."

"Isn't the guy next door a cop?" Tuck asked Paige.

She nodded. "Yes. Officer Leo Clark. But we can't call *him*. He's a nice guy, but he'd probably feel it was his duty to tell our folks the minute they pulled into the driveway."

"We'd better hope he doesn't hear all this racket then," Katie murmured nervously. Sounds from within the house gathered volume.

"He won't. It's not as if his house is right on top of ours. There's a big yard and garden separating the two houses, and the windows are closed in both of them. He's probably not home, anyway. They usually go out on Saturday nights."

"Well, while you decide what to do about the invasion of the house-snatchers," Paige said in a disgusted voice, "I'm going in there to make sure they haven't scared the wits out of Megan and Mary Emily."

"They're in bed, aren't they?" Katie asked as Paige turned to leave. "They're upstairs. Those people wouldn't go *upstairs,* would they?"

Paige gave her a look, said, "Oh, brother, you're unreal, Katie!" and went into the house.

"Oh, I don't believe any of this!" Katie cried. "This can't be happening! Tuck, *do* something!"

Tuck laughed, not a pleasant sound. "Oh, sure, Katie. Tell you what, I'll just saunter on in there and throw each person out bodily. I'll start with that hulk who is semi-attached to Jennifer. As long as you promise to come and visit me in the hospital when every bone in my body is broken."

"Katie," Sara said softly, "listen, I hate to do

this, but I think I'd better scram. If the police *do* come, I mean if the neighbors call the police or something, I don't want to be here. Does that make me a total rat?"

"Sara!" Lisa cried. "What's wrong with you? Of course it makes you a total rat! Listen, we're Katie's best friends, and she's in a jam here. How can you even think about deserting her at a time like this?" Diane nodded hearty agreement, but Katie felt sorry for Sara.

"It's okay, Sara," she said. "If you think you should go, it's okay. I understand."

Sara shook her head. "No, they're right. I shouldn't be thinking of myself right now. I'm sorry. I'll stay."

"Thanks. The trouble is, I really don't know what to do."

"Well," Ben said, "I don't know about anybody else, but we're not doing any good out here, so I'm going inside. Who knows what's happened to Paige. Maybe she's been trampled by that crowd."

The sound of breaking glass and an angry shout from Paige reassured them that she was still healthy enough to yell.

"We'd better get inside," Katie agreed, and they entered the raucous fray.

Upstairs, Paige was comforting Megan and Mary Emily. The noise downstairs had upset them. "Is Katie giving a party?" Mary Emily wanted to know. "Mother said not to."

As tempted as Paige was to blame Katie for the evening's events, she was convinced her stepsister had never invited these people. She wouldn't do that. Not after her mother had given her strict orders not to. The study group was one thing — this brawl quite another. But Paige would bet that Katie was at that moment wishing she'd never been born. Or, if she had to be born, that she certainly had never come up with the idea of "inviting a few friends in."

"No, Katie's not giving a party, honey. We've just got some pests downstairs we have to get rid of."

"They're making an awful lot of noise," Mary Emily said, her eyes wide. "They won't break my record player, will they?" It was in the playroom downstairs, and Paige knew better than to make any promises about its safety.

"I know they're too noisy, honey," she said, tucking Mary Emily's blanket about her stepsister's shoulders. "That's why we have to make them leave. Now, you two stay in your room, okay?" She didn't want to scare them, but she really felt it would be best if they didn't come downstairs. "I know you can't sleep because of all the noise, but you can talk or read. I'll be back up when things are back to normal. Soon, I promise. Okay?"

Megan and Mary Emily nodded as rock music began blaring throughout the house. "Gee," Megan said, "Tuck doesn't even turn his music up that loud. I bet they can hear that all the way downtown."

"Probably," Paige agreed dryly. "Well, don't you worry. We'll take care of it. Just stay here, right?"

They nodded again, and Paige left, closing the

149

door firmly behind her. She would personally clobber anyone who tried to make it up these stairs.

The first floor rocked with noise. A musical group wailed that no one understood them (which Paige felt was probably true because she knew *she* certainly didn't), people were scattered throughout the house laughing and shouting. It occurred to her as she made her way through the crowd to the playroom, the whole scene resembled a zoo.

The playroom was a shambles. After shooing away the people lounging on the old sofa and sitting on the floor against the wall, Paige took a good look around. She went first to Mary Emily's beloved record player, making a face of distaste when she saw it. Someone had poked a hole in the center of a pizza and impaled it on the metal spindle designed for centering spinning records. It oozed tomato sauce and melted cheese on and over the edges of the platform.

"Oh, gross!" Paige cried, and ran for a roll of paper towels from the kitchen. When she had done the best she could for the record player, she surveyed the rest of the room. Potato chips had been ground into the tile floor. Bathroom tissue had been unrolled along the entire length of the room and trailed along the back of the couch like road markings. All the younger girls' stuffed animals lay in a heap in one corner of the room. Mary Emily's and Megan's records had apparently been used as Frisbees and were scattered about the room, some on the floor, some on the furniture, some lying in the hall outside the room.

Paige clenched her teeth and headed for the kitchen.

She found Katie conferring with Ben, Tuck, and Katie's friends about what to do. They were surrounded by party-goers who were laughing and shouting and, in some cases, tossing food, an act that seemed to strike them as hilarious. Katie and her cohorts huddled in a corner, trying to make themselves heard over the racket.

"I don't understand," Katie moaned in a bewildered voice as Paige pushed her way into their small circle, "I don't even know most of these people. What are they doing here?"

"They're partying," Lisa said in a matter-of-fact voice. "They found out your parents weren't home, and that was all they needed to know. They don't need to know *you*."

"You should consider yourself lucky," Sara added. The sound of smashing glass made her pause before saying, "I was just going to say at least they haven't broken anything valuable. I hope that sound we just heard wasn't any of your mom's good crystal. There was another party right here in Philadelphia last year where the kids did twenty thousand dollars worth of damage, no kidding. They broke just about everything in the house, including smashing the toilets and punching holes in the walls."

"Sara!" Diane scolded. "Quit scaring her. These kids aren't going to do anything like that."

Sara shrugged.

Paige was wondering about something. She had assumed it was Katie who had let slip the information that they were temporarily parentless. But she was remembering now Deirdre's interest in her conversation at school.

"Anybody seen that Deirdre-person?" she asked casually. The noise level in the kitchen had decreased slightly as the food-throwers took their sporting event elsewhere. "You know the one I mean, the one who's trying desperately to give leather a bad name?" A paper plate flew by her and landed in a sink already filled with soggy cups, soggy potato chips, crumpled paper napkins, some in the form of airplanes, and a pile of golden metal caps that Paige knew hadn't come from bottles of soft drinks.

"Yeah," Diane answered, making a face to show her opinion of the leather-clad Deirdre. "She's here with a real scuzzball named George. Why?"

"No reason. I just wondered." So. It was almost certain then that this party was the result of her *own* big mouth, not Katie's. Well, she couldn't do anything about that now. Deirdre shouldn't have been eavesdropping, anyway. If it was anyone's fault, it was Deirdre's. Not that she was likely to care, or to feel the least bit remorseful about what was happening to Paige's home.

A resounding crash from the direction of the library brought all of them to attention. "Oh, no!" Katie said softly. "I'm afraid to go see what that was." But she went, followed by the others. To find one of the tall bookcases lying, facedown, on the library floor.

"I think it's dead," a chunky boy in a plaid shirt said solemnly. He grabbed a large white vase full of fall flowers from an end table and dumped its contents on the bookcase. "I now pronounce you decently buried," he said, and laughed hilariously. Then he left the room, lurching slightly as he walked. Water from the vase dripped across the bookshelves and onto the hardwood floor.

"Look at this room!" Paige cried. There were books scattered everywhere, many sprawled, spine side up with their pages crumpled underneath them. More bathroom tissue was wound around the drapery rods and trailed down the sides of the windows. All of the paintings Virginia Mae was so fond of had been turned toward the wall. Crushed chips and peanuts layered the floor, mixed with small puddles of water where tossed ice cubes had melted.

"The piano!" Paige cried. "Tuck, check the piano. I'm afraid to."

"It's okay," he said a moment later. "But your sheet music looks like it's been trampled by a herd of elephants."

Paige rushed to his side. It was true. Her collection of music, as well as Virgina Mae's, had been scattered all along the back of the room.

A girl in high heels and tight black pants wandered into the room. "Is this the bathroom?" she asked in a sleepy voice.

"Of course!" Paige snapped. "Why else would there be a piano in here?"

The girl stared blankly at her. "Right," she said. But a moment later she murmured, "Gee, I don't think I need a piano," and turned and left the room.

Tuck followed her, located the stereo, and turned down the volume. There were shouts of protest and seconds later, as he hurried back to the library, someone else turned it back up. Passing the kitchen, he noticed with irritation that the refrigerator door stood open, a fact everyone in the crowded room was ignoring. Pushing his way toward it, he slammed it shut, and wished fervently that he had a padlock. He sensed that it would be open again before he'd made his way back out of the room.

A girl in a yellow sweatsuit was writing on the stove top with a tube of bright red lipstick. Without a word, Tuck yanked the lipstick from her hand and stormed out of the room, her indignant, "Hey, whadya think you're doing?" ringing in his ears.

Striding straight through the mess, Tuck shouted at a group of people lounging on the stairs, "You people are pigs, you know that? And I'm probably insulting the pigs by saying that!"

There were hoots, boos, and catcalls as he entered the library, but he didn't care. Enough was enough!

Katie was crying when he reached the small group, helping Paige in her attempts to regroup the music sheets. "Oh, Tuck," Katie said as he bent to help them, "what are we going to do? We *have* to call the police, there's just no other way."

"Tuck. Tuck?" He looked up to see Jennifer standing in the doorway. Her face was almost as pale as Katie's, her brown eyes wide as she focused on the room's appearance. "Oh, Tuck," she said softly, "I'm so sorry."

"Why?" he asked, acid in his voice. "Did you do this?" He had never been so angry with any-

154

one. There she stood, looking perfectly beautiful in a pale-blue blouse and jeans, and the fact was, she was part of all this! Why? She wasn't like the others, he knew she wasn't. She couldn't be. He wasn't sure how he felt about her anymore, or how he would feel about her later, but right now, he was furious with her.

"Well, no, I didn't do it, but . . ." She moved on into the room, and a group of people gathered behind her in the doorway. "But it really is inexcusable. This . . . this awful mess!"

"I *know* it's inexcusable. I wasn't planning on excusing anyone." He looked directly at her, his anger refusing to wane. "Were you?"

Her eyes avoided his, focusing instead on the recently-deceased bookcase. "I didn't know we were coming here, Tuck, honest. I don't think most of the kids did. We just heard there was a party, so . . ."

"Party?" Tuck's sisters and friends, sensing his fury, remained silent, letting him be their spokesperson. "You call this a party? In Atlanta, this would be considered trespassing. Which, at least in Atlanta, is considered against the law. In fact, from what I've seen so far, it would also be considered vandalism. You know, the kind of stunt criminals pull!"

Scarlet flooded Jennifer's pale cheeks. More people had gathered in the doorway, and someone had turned down the stereo. Every word Tuck uttered rang through the room.

"None of you were invited here," he continued. "And on top of that, you're all behaving like . . ." he hated saying these things to her, but someone

155

had it coming and it might as well be her. She was with them, wasn't she? "like animals. Now," he added, "I understand why you and your friends make fun of my southern manners. It's because you have no manners of your own."

Another crash, this one from the kitchen, broke the awkward silence that followed Tuck's outburst.

"Okay, that does it!" Ben cried. He rushed out of the room, pushing through the crowd in the doorway and ran down the hallway. Paige, Tuck, and Katie and her friends followed.

The kitchen looked worse than the library. There was food everywhere, on the floor, on the counters, on the table and chairs. The sink was piled high with trash, two of the chairs were upended and someone had written LIFE STINKS on the refrigerator door with what looked like grape juice.

"Oh," Katie said, stunned. And again, "Oh."

"I wish I had my camera," Ben said grimly. "I'd photograph this mess and show the photos around school on Monday. Maybe I'd even put it in the paper. Because most of these people aren't going to believe us when we tell them what they did tonight."

"This is *your* party," Paige cried angrily, facing Katie. "Why don't you *do* something?"

"It's *not* my party!" Katie shouted, her cheeks flaming, tears sparkling in her eyes. "I never invited any of these people, and you know it!"

"Maybe not, but you invited your own friends over. Virginia Mae is never going to believe you didn't just invite the whole school, and *you* know that!"

Katie's face drained of all color and for just a moment, Paige felt sorry for her. Then she remembered Katie's superiority during the past week, her smugness when Paige had performed some stupid little household chore the wrong way, and she said, "Why don't you just make your delicious omelettes for everyone and then maybe they'll go home?"

Katie burst into tears. Someone rapped on the back door and when Tuck opened it, Jake came into the kitchen.

"Well," he said to Katie, ignoring her tear-stained face, "no wonder you didn't want me to come over tonight. You're having a party."

"I'M NOT HAVING A PARTY!" she shouted, swiping at her tears with the sleeve of her sweater. "For the *last* time, I am *not* having a party!"

Paige made up her mind quickly. As satisfying as it was to see Katie in trouble, this was *her* house, too. She had no intention of standing by quietly while it was reduced to rubble. And it really wasn't all that great to see Katie so upset. It didn't make Paige feel all warm and nice inside, the way she might have thought it would. It made her feel uncomfortable, as if her wool sweater were too tight or too itchy.

Without a word, she slipped out of the house and ran across the yard, with only the lights from the house to guide her, until she reached Officer Leo Clark's back porch. When he answered her frantic knock a few moments later, he was in uniform, which she hadn't expected. A big, burly man with ruddy cheeks, he smiled down at Paige. She had known him ever since she was a child and she liked and trusted him.

"Well, hello, Paige! Your timing is perfect. We just returned from a banquet. Five minutes earlier, and you'd have missed us. What's up? I guess you're having a party over at your place, hmm? We heard party sounds when we got out of the car."

"Officer Clark, I hate to bother you," she began awkwardly, "but we're not really *having* a party. That is, we aren't supposed to be. Our parents are out of town, and word got out, and all these people, well, they just sort of descended on us and . . ."

He lifted one bushy eyebrow. "Don't tell me, let me guess. Uninvited guests, right?"

"Right! And these people, they're from school so we didn't want to call the police, you know? But they're making a mess of the house and we have to get them out of there."

"Say no more." Taking her by the elbow, he began leading her down the steps and across the lawn. "I'm an old hand at this sort of thing. Don't you worry about a thing. Let me handle it, okay?"

She nodded and hurried to keep up with his long strides. "Um, Officer Clark, we were under strict orders not to have anybody in the house while our folks were gone. And we really didn't intend to. If they find out about this, we'll all be grounded until doomsday. And it wasn't our fault, honest!"

"Relax, Paige," the big man said as they reached the garden gate and rock music greeted their ears. "I'll do my duty and then I'll go home. You did the right thing by coming to me about this, so I don't think your folks need to know."

She looked up at him. "You mean you're not going to tell them?"

"Not unless they ask me." They had reached the back steps. "So your job," he said as they climbed the steps, "will be to dispose of all the evidence so that your folks have no reason to ask me."

Paige nodded. But she was thinking, Disposing of the evidence should be Katie's job. *She's* the one who broke the rule and invited people here, even if it was only a few friends and not the whole school. Let *her* clean up the mess!

Paige wondered afterward if the sight of Officer Leo Clark in a plain gray suit would have had the same impact as the sight of Officer Leo Clark in a policeman's uniform. Probably not, she decided.

Mouths dropped open, groans of disbelief issued forth, people stopped what they were doing, which was mostly throwing food, and stared as Officer Clark entered the kitchen. Katie, still at the sink with Jake, Ben, and Tuck and Katie's friends, gave a hefty sigh that Paige couldn't interpret. Was it dismay? Or relief? She decided it didn't matter. Help was here, whether Katie liked it or not.

The big policeman made his way from room to room, leaving silence in his wake. There were protests, some of them shouted. But no one was willing to tangle with a grizzly bear in uniform.

"Aw, Whitman!" Ed Thomas called, "what'd you go and call the law for? We were just having a party!" But the shambles that had been created out of the Whitman living room proved to Officer Clark that Paige had definitely made the right move in calling for his help.

"Okay, folks!" he called as he strode through the house with Paige right behind him, "Party's over! Everybody out! Any people still in here in ten minutes hand over their school I.D.s and I phone their parents."

What had been, just moments before, a rowdy, wall-shaking cacophony of music, laughter, and shouts, rapidly became an uneasy silence broken only by some muttered grumbling.

"We didn't do anything," a blonde girl sprawled on the living room couch, now minus its cushions, said sullenly. "We were just having fun."

"I can see that," Officer Clark said dryly, surveying the chaos. "Well, fun's over for tonight. Let's move it on out of here."

There was one long moment then when Paige held her breath. It didn't look as if anyone intended to move. She hadn't formulated a Plan B. Would Officer Clark have to call in reinforcements? Visions of an entire police squad running up the front steps made her shudder.

But Leo Clark wasn't giving an inch. "Out!" he commanded in a deep, no-nonsense voice, "Now!"

Slowly, too slowly to suit Paige, several girls got to their feet and stood there uncertainly, waiting for a move from the boys. She could tell the boys were torn between a need to stand their ground and a fear of tangling with the officer. Fear won out, and she heaved a sigh of relief as one by one, the boys unwound themselves from various positions on the floor and the furniture, and stood up. Once that move had been made, the next logical step seemed to be to obey Officer Clark's orders and give up the party altogether. Shrugging, grumbling, delivering looks of disgust toward Paige, the living room crowd began to amble from the room, shouting to other groups in other rooms to join them as they made their way to the front door.

When it had, at long last, closed on the last of them, Paige, Tuck, and Katie thanked the policeman profusely. "I don't know how we would have chased them out of here without your help," a pale-faced Katie told him, shaking his hand.

"No problem," he said, smiling down at her. "Your sister here did the right thing, coming to me. Crowds like that can be a real handful."

Paige looked smug.

"And I promise," he added as he left by the back door, "this is between you people and me *unless* your folks ask me. See that they don't, okay?"

They promised, and he left.

Katie's knees gave, and she sank into a chair, putting her head in her hands. "I can't believe they're gone," she moaned. "And I can't believe this happened! It's like a nightmare!"

Jake patted her shoulder. "Well, it's all over now. Relax. They're gone."

They hadn't been gone more than a few minutes when the phone rang. Paige frowned. "Don't tell me one of the neighbors is calling to complain about the noise *now*," she said, and picked up the telephone. Then her face went chalk-white as she cried, "Dad! Why are you calling? We just talked to you today. Is anything wrong?" The kitchen fell totally silent as everyone stopped what they were doing to listen. Paige was stricken by a terrible sense that her father could see straight through the telephone into the disaster that was his home.

"You're *what*?" Her eyes, large and dark, met Katie's. "You're coming home *tomorrow*?"

CHAPTER 16

No one in the room said a word. They stood stock-still in the kitchen and listened to Paige's end of the telephone conversation.

"I don't understand why you're coming home," Paige said. "I mean, you were having such a great time! We weren't expecting you until Wednesday." Scanning the room that she was sure would take at least seven years of hard work to get back to normal, she closed her eyes in misery. "You're leaving there *tonight*?" Paige's voice rose. Katie clutched at Jake's arm. Tuck groaned. "Arriving at Kennedy in the morning? *Sunday* morning? Well, yes, I know about the time difference, but . . ."

"No, no, no!" Katie murmured, "they can't come home tomorrow, they can't! If they do, I'm dead!"

Paige coughed suddenly, and her cheeks reddened. "Well, of course we want you to come home!"

Katie shook her head vigorously. Ignoring her, Paige said, "It's just that we wanted you to have more time, that's all. Sure. Sure. Okay. See you then. Have a good trip. 'Bye!"

She replaced the receiver slowly, as if by stalling her actions she could somehow change the message it had delivered. Then she lifted her head and looked directly at Katie. "That's it, we're dead!" she said flatly. "You heard. They'll be arriving at Kennedy tomorrow around eight o'clock. So, barring hurricanes or major floods in New York, they'll be pulling into our driveway in a cab sometime around noon."

"No," Katie moaned, "oh, no!"

"They got homesick when they talked to us this afternoon." And hadn't that telephone call been *her* idea? Great! All she needed in this life was a little more guilt. "So they decided to cut their visit short."

"Bad timing?" Jake asked Katie quietly, surveying the kitchen.

Katie nodded. "There is no way," she said dully, "that we can get this entire house shipshape that fast."

"Sure, we can," Jake said cheerfully, "if everyone helps."

"You don't understand, Jake," Sara said. "It's not just this room. The whole first floor looks like this."

"So? That means we're home free with the second and third floors, right?"

"Well, count me out," Paige announced, standing up. "This wasn't *my* idea. *I* didn't let the animals out of the zoo and into my house."

164

"Neither did *I*," Katie said defensively.

"Paige," Jake said patiently, "does it really matter how they all got here? The fact is, we need *seven* able-bodied people to pull the pieces back together."

Sara, Lisa, and Diane exchanged uneasy glances. "I'll stay as long as I can," Sara said quietly. "But I have a curfew, Katie, and I'll have to get home on time. It's already pretty late." Lisa and Diane nodded.

"I know," Katie said wearily. "When you're ready, Tuck will drive you home. All of you."

"But we'll work like crazy till then," Lisa said quickly. "This isn't much worse than cleaning up after a prom, and we all did that last year, right, girls?"

Sara and Diane grimaced. "We sure did. Although," Diane added slowly, "we didn't have to clean a kitchen."

"I'll take the kitchen," Katie offered. "You guys hit the playroom and the library, okay? Just do what you can until you have to leave."

The three girls left as Ben moved over to Paige's side. "When they go home," he said quietly, "that will only leave the four of us. You're not really going to cop-out, are you?"

Paige bent down to remove an orange peel from the bottom of her shoe. "I'm tired," she said, "aren't you?"

Katie heard her and burst out, "Well, it's your own fault you're tired! You shouldn't have stayed out all night!"

A shocked silence filled the room for the second time in twenty minutes. Katie clapped a hand over her mouth, regretting her words. Jake stared at Paige and Ben. Paige's face turned a deep, angry red and her dark eyes aimed a look of sheer hatred at her stepsister. Tuck asked his sister, "Why didn't you tell me? I didn't know she didn't come home last night."

"I *did* come home!" Paige snapped. "If I hadn't, I wouldn't be standing here now, would I?"

"So where were you all night?" Tuck was very annoyed with Paige. If their parents found out, he'd be held responsible. Hadn't Bill put him in charge?

"Battery died on me," Ben answered for Paige. "We'd taken a short-cut and there wasn't anyone around to jump it for me, so we had to wait until morning." He made it sound so logical that the shock drained out of Jake's and Tuck's faces.

Tuck looked at Katie. "You made it sound so sinister," he accused. "They just had car trouble. You can't jump a battery if there's no other car around."

"Well, Paige never bothered to explain any of that to *me*," Katie said harshly. "I guess she thought I didn't deserve an explanation even though I waited up for her most of the night." Then, to Paige, she added, "And I don't see why you should be any more tired than me!"

"Well," Paige said, "I *am*. And I *don't* clean up other people's messes!"

Tuck laughed. "Are you kidding? You don't even clean up your own! But this is an emergency and it involves the whole family and if you don't help, then I don't think you care about this family at all!"

"That is *not* true!" Paige insisted. "I do care!"

"Well, then?"

Paige felt all eyes on her. And she knew she was going to give in. Because she wouldn't be able to sleep, anyway, with so much activity going on down here. Because a person would have to have a heart of stone not to feel sympathy for Katie at this particular moment. And I don't, she thought, bending to pick up a can of soda, have a heart of stone. It may be solidified some days, but it's not stone. And most of all, she was going to give in because she didn't want Jake and Tuck and Ben looking at her as if she'd just crawled out from under a rock. Especially Ben.

"Okay, okay," she said. "You're right, okay? It's my house, too. Now that the barbarians have gone in search of other battlefields to conquer, we survivors might as well start rebuilding."

Katie sighed with relief and the boys relaxed. "But I'm *not*," Paige added, looking around the kitchen, "taking *this* room. I still have aches and pains from mopping up pudding."

Katie laughed weakly. "I'll do this room. You and Ben take the living room. Jake and Tuck can help me out here."

Sara and Diane and Lisa were true to their word and had worked wonders in the playroom and library by the time they left the house. Katie thanked them profusely and they all gave her a hug of reassurance. "It'll be okay," Diane whispered as she left. "Don't worry, okay? It'll turn your hair gray."

Laughing, Katie closed the door after them.

With Tuck gone to drive the girls home, Katie and Jake were alone in the kitchen, which was slowly beginning to look like a kitchen again.

Jake joined Katie at the kitchen sink. Taking her by the arms, he turned her around to face him. "You have to listen to me," he said firmly.

"Jake!" She wouldn't look at him. "I've got to get done here!"

"You will. I'll help. But first, I want you to listen to me because I can't stand that look on your face anymore."

"What look?" she asked wearily.

"*That* look. The one that says I stuck a knife into you. I didn't *mean* to." He shook his head. "You're always so up, so cheerful, I forget sometimes how . . . how easily you get hurt."

"I'm *not* fragile, Jake!"

"I didn't say that. I know you're not. But your feelings are awfully close to the surface. If I'd had any idea you would be in that restaurant that night, I'd have called you ahead of time and told you what my dad had asked me to do. Can't you just accept my apology so we can go on from there?"

Katie Summer's pride was strong. But she was tired. And she had missed Jake. And the memory of that Sunday night was rapidly fading because of everything else that had happened during the past week. And the girl hadn't been all that pretty, anyway.

So she walked into Jake Carson's arms and stayed there until the last of her hurt and anger were gone.

*　*　*

In the library, Ben handed Paige the last of the disheveled books and she placed it on the upright shelves.

"How come you didn't tell Katie exactly what happened?" he said as Paige looked around the room to see what their next task should be.

"Oh, Ben. I don't want to talk about that now."

"Well, I do." Taking her elbow, he turned her around to face him. "You could have straightened out the whole thing right away, and you didn't. I want to know why."

Paige sank down onto the couch, its pillows restored to their proper places. "I don't know," she admitted softly. "I should have." Ben sat down beside her, placing an arm around her shoulders. "And I wanted to, at first. But when she acts like she's older than I am, like she's my *mother*, it makes me crazy! And I get . . ."

"Stubborn?" he asked gently, a smile on his face.

Good. That meant he wasn't really mad. He was just curious about her motives, and she couldn't blame him for that. It must be hard for him to understand this weird relationship she had with Katie Summer.

She nodded. "Yeah, I guess."

"And you've learned your lesson and it won't ever happen again, right?"

She knew he was probably grinning like crazy, but she glanced over at him just to make sure. He was. "Right," she said, returning the grin, "and peace and love shall reign supreme in the

169

Whitman-Guthrie household from this moment on."

He laughed. "You don't mind if I don't hold my breath waiting for that to happen, do you?"

She would have laughed, too, but she couldn't because he was kissing her.

They finished cleaning up in the small hours of the morning. Jake and Ben went home, and the girls and Tuck managed to grab a few hours of sleep before they were awakened by Megan and Mary Emily. The two younger girls pitched in to help and put the finishing touches on the clean-up job. Afterward, Katie fixed them all a big breakfast. And during the meal, a sleepy, cranky Tuck wanted to know what they were going to tell their parents about the unexpected, unplanned "party."

"I really don't think we should tell them anything," Paige said. "It happened, we cleaned up the mess, and it's over. I just don't see any point in telling them."

"For once," Katie said with a relieved smile, "I agree with you totally, Paige."

"Ditto," Tuck mumbled. "But what about the small fry?" glancing toward Megan and Mary Emily.

"Megan?" Paige asked in the same tone of voice she would have used with an adult, "do you think we should tell Virginia Mae and Dad what happened last night?"

Megan shook her head firmly. "Nope. They're going to be upset enough about Miss Aggie's accident."

Katie groaned. "Oh, no, I forgot! We thought Miss Aggie would be back here before Mom and Dad, but she won't be. Mom's going to have a fit!"

"I think," Mary Emily offered, "that we should wait and tell them about last night some other time. Maybe after they've been back for a while."

"Agreed," Paige said firmly. "We'll save that one for later."

"I just hope Mom doesn't get crazy when she finds out about Miss Aggie's fall," Katie said.

Virginia Mae did, indeed, "get crazy" when she learned that they had been alone most of the week. "I can't believe," she cried, sinking into a living room chair that, just hours earlier, had been sprawled upside-down in a corner, "that you didn't call us immediately and tell us! We'd have come straight home!"

"That's why we didn't call," Tuck said. His foot had just accidentally discovered a soda can peeking out from under the couch and he was busy unobtrusively pushing it backward, out of sight.

"Look," Bill Whitman said to his wife, "they're fine. Aren't they? They certainly look fine. And the house looks fine, too. Isn't that proof that they're old enough and capable enough to take care of themselves? They were thinking of us, not wanting to spoil our trip. I'm proud of them, and I think you should be, too."

"You're right," Virginia Mae said after a moment, a smile creasing her face. "You're absolutely right. And I think instead of discussing this now, you should hand me that shopping bag over there so we can show these wonderful offspring of ours that we were thinking of them while we were in Hawaii."

Because she was talking, she never heard the collective sigh of relief coming from the Whitman-Guthrie clan.

Paige and Katie opened their gifts. At one point, they each looked up at the same time and their eyes met. Katie's glance said, I didn't tell about your breaking curfew.

And Paige's said, And I didn't tell about your "party." And then her eyes said quite clearly, But the party was worse than the curfew and I helped you clean up after it. So you owe me one. And I, dear *step*sister, intend to collect.

If Katie really loves Jake, why is she making a play for the handsome new soccer star? Read Stepsisters #5, THAT CHEATING SISTER.